This novella is dedicated to m̲   ̲vas the bravest, most courageous person I know. She changed her behaviour out of her love for me. She was 86! A testament to those who think it's sometimes too late to change. I will always cherish the times spent during the last four months of my grandma's life.

To Jayne
with love Marcus xx

Acknowledgements

Firstly I'd like to thank Stephen Lyons, not just for proofreading, but for always allowing an authentic space so as to connect, regardless of how daring or awkward. Thank you!

Massive gratitude to Emily Sharpe for her generous, kind spirit and her continued practical advice, support and love. Thanks for reading my first creative material and for your invaluable feedback, but mostly thanks for choosing me as your best friend.

Thanks to Nicolas Normand for his continued love, encouragement and attention and always supporting me in my growth. I am so lucky to have two best friends!

Thanks to Dave and Emma, also for their continued love and support in various areas of my life. I will never forget it.

Thanks to Craig Ryder who never fails to inspire me by continually bringing people together, but mostly for his unquenching appetite to grab life and fully own every situation with an innate grace. Thanks for having me in your life.

And last but not least, thanks to Tari Fante, my little sister, for her openness and laughs but mostly for being so, so courageous. Love you!

To everyone in my life who aren't afraid of connecting authentically. This book could not have been created without you! Thank you!

"We are meaning-seeking creatures who must deal with the inconvenience of being hurled into a universe that intrinsically has no meaning."

Irvin Yalom

INFORMANTS

This is a story about learning to play with the cards we've been given. A story about how to see, truly see what's right in front of us without using our 'filter' which only lets us see the 'imprint' of our past.

It's a tale about all the wonderful things we do every day to embrace our humanness and of how we save each other every day mostly without knowing; allowing for a connectedness that is life...a life worth living.

1

Giles sits in his favourite armchair in the hallway upstairs and contemplates the new book he is about to write. He loves this particular spot in the mornings because of the natural light which floods in from a skylight above; but more so because of an oak bookstand situated just in reach. This allows him to pick random books so as to fish for ideas when writing.

Adding to his admiration for this part of the house are the contrasting colours on the walls. Subconsciously however, he likes this area because of the unusual positioning. The chair blocks the entry to the bathroom and this probably epitomises his life. Plonking himself deliberately in awkward situations, immersing in a mindset only to sabotage his existence. But somehow refusing to move; a hard concept to accept but yes he purposely clings to a damaging mindset because that is what he's familiar with. Anxiety and fear flush addictive chemicals through his bloodstream and this is what he needs. Owning this fact is of course hard to muster. The amount of self help books on his solid oak bookstand attempts to shatter this fact.

Giles has always been drawn to self development and reading anything positive, empowering and soul sustaining. This keeps him moving forward as otherwise his corrupted mesh of neurons proclaiming to be his brain will surely get the better of him. So despite his trauma driven psyche, which manifests his existence. His perseverance to live a powerful more positive life also pushes through, creating a lovely conflict of emotions and state of being, which I guess when you think about it is purely natural.

Atoms have to have a negative and positive charge and repel and attract as their way of being and since we're all just atoms at the end of the day, why should conflict in our lives be a surprise? Our suffering is only exacerbated when we try to fight this natural state. Chaos is required; it is a natural play in the universe.

Giles sits and tries to meditate, he closes his eyes and takes in a deep breath and exhales slowly. Then he repeats the process again and again trying desperately to slow down his racing mind. He cannot remember how many books he has read on the subject of meditation – they all make being with your breath alone seem so easy. He finds it easier when he is focusing his mind on a task, like cooking or writing, sometimes gardening but seldom. Generally he has to be 'doing' so as to be present, even sitting to watch a film can be challenging as his mind wanders exhaustingly from thought to thought. Then his mind locks onto something to ruminate and wallow in, at which stage, he starts to chew his fingers.

He has also read a lot of books about acceptance. So he tries to balance learning to be a better version of himself everyday whilst accepting on some level he is an over thinking, lost and tortured soul and that is part of who he is. Owning this fact sometimes gave him the most immense peace but it never lasted, he would become self conscious and could see himself in the peaceful state and try to intellectualize it and of course whatever had arisen would quickly dissipate. Peacefulness like love does not like being observed in this way; just like the quantum wave function collapses when observed, so too does the state of love and peace and happiness for that matter. Even quantum physicists do not know why this is the case so no fat chance Giles would have a clue. The good news is that the negative emotions and thoughts when observed closely also disappear eventually. The problem is that most people would rather escape into any sort of activity rather than be with a feeling or thought they did not like.

Giles typically feels more alive when he's connected with another like minded person. He soaks these moments up, never wanting them to end. In some kind of warped irony, mostly when alone, his mind is overly active, principally as an attempt to reduce the malaise caused by an inner turmoil which only exacerbates his sense of aloneness and the illusion of being separated from everything else.

He remembers reading somewhere that this phenomenon is due to the way our minds work. Our minds form their ideas about reality by splitting it up into fragments cognitively, and then tries to reassemble those fragments into a model which it can understand. This is an inevitable process of natural and universal loss and what is lost is a sense of wholeness or unity which underlies reality.

Giles thinks to himself. "So there you have it – we're doomed because of the way our mind works and actually it seems the more cognitive ability you possess, the more fucked you are! Druggie hipsters may actually have known the answer all along. Getting high thus switching off our cognitive function may be the closest we are ever going to get to sensing oneness with everyone except if you maybe join a monastery! This shouldn't be disheartening, no quite the contrary it should help everyone 'chillax' because we are programmed in this chaotic way. Embrace the chaos!"

Giles checks the time on his phone and stretches whilst getting up. He has an interview today for a new job and he's particularly pleased he's not overly attached to getting the job. He would like a change but he's also happy with his present job, he just wishes to weigh up the options.

He is a writer and often works from home except when he has to interview people for a particular article or book. He's interested in using his writing skills to work for a charitable organisation, perhaps working in their administrative sector creating marketing blogs. He had worked for Oxfam when he had been temping, which he did for months whilst finding his feet, (more like finding his mind in his case). He hadn't known from week to week or month to month whether he would have a job or not and this somehow made him feel more alive. "Uncertainty" it would seem is just as pleasing to our human condition as "certainty" was, if not more so in some cases. A subconscious craving for the chaos perhaps?

Giles knows from past experiences that to be too attached to anything causes him to perform poorly. A healthy balance of nonchalance and determination is what is required and he felt he was comfortably in this space, so he was happy.

Being too attached is like trying to grasp onto water, it just seeps from your fingers. He once wrote a metaphor in one of his books about someone being able to freeze water by exhaling an icy breath, (water symbolises anything you were trying to hold onto), like one of the X men, thus turning it to ice and then being able to hold onto it firmly. If only we could do this with those notable moments so they didn't end. If only we could do that with love or peace, grasping onto it for dear life. Of course it didn't work that way. Love and peace are like the quantum wave. These euphoric states of being flow and all we can do, indeed all we must do, is immerse ourselves without attachment and be present in the enjoyment, without observing intellectually, because the state would be sure to collapse. Why were we given minds you may ask? No mind – instant peace! He remembers something he wrote in another book while watching a Pigeon take flight upwards, flapping her wings frantically to gain height and then soaring downwards, swerving and gliding as it decreased altitude. Watching this bird conjured up a sense of freedom and peace and he thought to himself, "Now there's a creature without a mind." At times he would sit and listen to 'Lark Ascending' by Ralph Vaughn Williams just to heighten the feeling when reminiscing about the bird. This piece of music always guaranteed tears of joy, and it reminded him that if he hadn't endured in his early life he would not have the profound connection he had with the music. He knew all too well, that the deeper; sadness is carved into our being, the more joy we are able to hold, if we let it.

Giles knows that without the mind we would not appreciate magical moments either, for in order to appreciate those moments we have to be aware of the opposite, hence the paradox.

 He gets up and moves the arm chair slightly so he can access the bathroom. He smirks as he does so, it's a subconscious smirk which he does automatically now through habit, completely unaware. He switches the bathroom light on. Although a big frosted window is in the bathroom, an old Oak in the garden, possibly with a tree preservation order on, blocks out most of the light. He gets his clothes off and is about to hop into the bath (well not hop, more like lifting one leg and placing it in the bath and then lifting the other leg. Gone were the days of him hopping into anything.) He's about to turn the shower on when the doorbell goes.

'Typical.' he mutters under his breath and climbs back out again grabbing his bathrobe from the hook on the door and wraps it around himself. The doorbell goes again and he mutters again to himself. 'Coming, coming...impatient bugger.'

He manoeuvres himself around the armchair resisting a smirk. He moves swiftly down the stairs and peeps through the door viewer. He can't see anything at first and then out of his peripheral vision appears a woman with tattered clothes. He is quite sure he can make out small splatters of blood on her dress, unless it was the design of the material. His heart races a little as he opens the door.

'Please help me.' The lady mumbles wiping away tears from her eyes.

'What happened?' Giles asks through slight palpitations in his chest.

He has always suffered with anxiety and he had several theories to why he struggled with this sometimes dilapidating mental state. The fact he was epileptic did not help matters, because he was always frightened the anxiety would trigger a seizure. The irony was despite these mental setbacks he somehow still managed to deal with big challenges in life. Nonetheless, confronting people with issues and having to disclose or face any difficult intercourse are what often gave him anxiety tremors.

He scans the environment and sees no one else. He lives down a cul-de-sac and this unfortunately made his area more attractive to vandals or burglary. His next door neighbour was once robbed in broad daylight and he took measures to protect his home after that. He installed a secret camera on a pillar covered in ivy which had full coverage of his cul-de-sac. Not because he was particularly worried about things being stolen from his home, he didn't have anything that valuable and he never kept wads of cash at home. He just didn't like the idea of someone breaking in and rummaging through his home; almost in the same vain as the persistent rummaging which went on in his mind.

He was glad he was not materialistic. His father had unknowingly taught him from an early age that material wealth was no guarantee to happiness. His father was wealthy and abused him and his mother physically and emotionally and so he presupposed his dad couldn't have been overjoyed despite his material wealth. Buying him toys and all sorts of goods was the one way his dad used to show that he loved him. All Giles desperately wanted however and never got was a hug.

'Come in, come in.' Giles says with some trepidation.

'Thank you.' The lady mutters and ambles into the house.

'Please sit down.' Giles gestures to the seats in the living room. His living room and kitchen are open plan and spacious. The decor is contemporary modern, with an array of pictures of friends and holiday shots from around the world.

'My name is Giles, what happened?' Giles engineers calm.

'Thanks Giles, my name is Pa...Paula, thanks for letting me into your home.' Paula peers round the living room.

'Quite okay, what happened?'

'This is going to sound strange.' Paula glances at the floor for a few seconds and then returns her gaze to Giles.

'Who did this to you?' Giles scans her tattered clothes covered in blood stains.

'Are you hurt anywhere?'

'No...not that I can see anyway.' Paula checks herself.

Giles detects what appears to be a deep cut on her hand. It still bleeds a little and he presupposes the small platters of blood on her dress could have come from her hand.

'I really don't think I'm hurt.'

Giles wonders if she can't feel the cut on her hand or she doesn't think it's a big deal.

Paula touches herself and proceeds to check her groin which makes Giles uncomfortable and he turns away briefly.

'No...definitely not hurt.'

She stares at him as if daydreaming, she gapes straight through him. An uncomfortable silence ensues which makes Giles even more anxious. Not only the silence; there is now something about Paula he hadn't perceived before as she stood at his front door. He can't quite put a finger on it but she does not look authentic somehow. His stomach churns with the malaise as he struggles to be in this disquieted space.

'Can you tell me what happened?' Giles tries desperately to act normal and dissipate his nervous energy.

'I can't.' Paula continues to look right through Giles.

'Wh-What do you mean?'

'I mean I can't, I can't remember.'

'Oh, okay...do you know how long you've been aware of the condition you're in now?' Giles cringes a little as he is frightfully aware of his choice of words, his nerves are getting the better of him.

'Not sure, not too sure how long I've been walking out there. I could tell you were in, as I saw the bathroom light come on and so decided to come here.'

Giles ponders how possible that was, this woman must have keen eyesight to spot a light come on in a room in daylight. Then again the weather was overcast and so it was quite possible Paula could have seen the light in the bathroom come on.

'Okay Paula, I'm glad you came here. Now I think we should call the police straight away.'

'No, no police!'

'Why...why not?'

'I'm not sure, but please don't call the police.' Paula fidgets in the chair.

'Okay, okay...what's the last thing you remember?

'I remember walking down the street.'

'This street?'

'Yes this street.'

'Do you remember anything before?'

'Remember a light, a very bright light.'

'Okay, anything else?'

'Not really, just this bright light, all around me.' Paula coughs for a few seconds. 'Blinding whiteness.'

'Would you like something to drink?' Giles is shocked at his lack of hospitality.

'A glass of water please.'

'Okay, sure.' Giles gets up and meanders over to the kitchen. The kitchen is small but the layout is thought-out, very 'IKEA.' All the space is utilised. The decor is warm lime green and lemon yellow. Pans and utensils hang from the ceiling, in amongst two plants which also appear to take their rightful positions. Cupboards and shelves are fitted in all the wall space and on the shelves are mostly herb plants and cookery books arranged neatly.

Giles opens one of the cupboards and fetches a glass and fills it with water from the tap.

'Tap water okay.' Giles questions prematurely.

'Yes...fine...thank you.'

Giles strides over and hands the glass of water to Paula.

'Thank you.' Paula delicately takes the glass and gulps the water down.

'Would you like another glass?'

'If you wouldn't mind.'

'Course not.' Giles takes the glass off Paula and returns to the kitchen to fetch another glass of water from the tap. He potters back and hands it to Paula who again takes the glass off him and gulps the water down.

'I'm so sorry; I should have asked if you wanted a drink earlier.'

'That's okay...I should have said.' Paula smiles.

Giles is relieved to see her smile, especially since he still couldn't put a finger on why something about Paula seemed weird. Her smile gave him a much needed respite from conjuring all sorts of stuff in his susceptible rummaging head.

'I should go; I've taken enough of your time.' Paula gets up and spins around to face the door.

'Hang on a second. What are you going to do? You are going to at least see a doctor. Maybe you have amnesia or suffer an absence of some kind.'

'Yes, I will go to my GP but I must return home first.'

'Okay, promise me, I know you don't know me but promise you will go and see your GP.' Giles has always ensured that his relationship to his word was unquestionable and he presupposed that everyone else were able to do the same. He had always lived by a quote from Goethe. "Treat a man as he is and he will remain as he is. But treat a man as he can and should be and he will become as he can and should be."

'Yes, I promise.'

She starts to walk to the door. Giles follows behind, and spots another small stain of blood on her dress by her bum. She must have wiped her hand on her bottom. He also notices a disrupted flashing connectivity on the router which is situated on a sideboard next to the front door.

Paula opens the door then turns around slowly.

'The mind is a funny thing, it's also a beautiful thing, we don't quite fathom it, we don't even know how to use it, but one day we will.' She turns back around and strolls off down the street leaving Giles standing at his front door dumbfounded by the divine words that had just been dispersed from this stranger's mouth.

2

Giles sits in his study, which is also his meditating room when he wants to sit somewhere else other than on the chair by the bathroom. There is an electric piano in the study as he likes to tinker with ivories every now and again. He enjoys composing random pieces of music. Having knowledge of scales gives him the tools to do this and he was grateful for learning this at piano lessons but he had chosen not to carry on with the grades. Principally because he was not motivated to learn a piece he did not like. Three options were available to learn in any exam so if you didn't like any of the three pieces you were scuppered. At least he thought so. Not doing exams, he could choose exactly what piece he'd like to learn and play piano for fun whilst being motivated to learn.

The study was the heart of his home and so the internal decor was even more important. He made sure an environment was created which induced not just thought but excellent thought and exceptional reasoning. He had a shade of purple on a feature wall were the piano was pressed up against and the rest of the walls were painted in a shade of light greyish lilac.

On the piano were sentimental pictures, on the left, a dog he had as a kid called Teddy, it had gotten run over by traffic whilst chasing his dad's car as he drove to work. He had loved this dog a lot and it was the first time he had experienced loss and what it meant to grieve. On the right was a picture of his best friend who was like his soul mate and he loved her very much. She had recently had a baby and so he didn't see much of her anymore but they both knew they were there for each other. And the final picture was of his mum standing with both him and his sister at a park bench in countryside. His mum had passed away to cancer when he turned twenty and this had changed his life forever and still had a hold on him. He was grateful though to his pained past as he believed it was a prerequisite to his creativity.

A fancy candle holder which was bought for his 30th is situated next to the photograph of his best friend with scented candles. He would often ignite the candle if he had a bloated tummy, as he was prone to smelly farts. When he was in the writing zone he didn't want any reason to leave his desk, not even his sometimes malodorous farts!

On the walls, were two pictures, a large one of Lyndsay Wagner who he adored as a kid. She starred as the Bionic Woman and he lost himself in these television series as a means to escape a traumatic childhood. On the opposite wall was a picture of a serene landscape of a lake surrounded by woodland.

Giles stretches whilst at his desk, and he gazes into his garden. He had purposely placed his desk by the window so he can do this. He admires his garden and day dreams. This is part of a ritual he does when writing. At first he used to beat himself up as he always labelled it as procrastination but after tormenting himself for months, he decided to accept the day dreaming as part of his process. He would always return to his laptop to start writing again eventually, often with full gusto. So what was the problem? Every writer must have their own ritual; he thought to himself. This was his.

He would sit most of the day, occasionally getting up to have something to eat. He didn't stick to meal times as such. He ate when he was hungry but often ate something healthy. He was conscious his work required use of his imagination and so he was fanatical about feeding his brain. For breakfast, he often had porridge and blueberries. He was always hungry around 11am and would often have sushi with added mackerel for lunch and for a snack always different kinds of nuts, largely macadamia and walnuts. He also ensured he drank at least 8 pints of water a day and he stuck to drinking two cups of coffee a day, one cup first thing in the morning and the other after he had his lunch. The second cup was to counter balance tiredness from all the blood going to his tummy for digestion purposes.

He had not been able to stop thinking about Paula who visited him first thing in the morning. She had made him late for his interview but he was partly pleased as he believed it was a sign not to bother. He had phoned the organisation and apologised saying he had changed his mind. The meeting with Paula was strange and what she said before leaving even stranger. What had she meant by what she said? Before the doorbell had rang he was contemplating before getting into the shower, what was the coincidence she would mention something profound about the mind before leaving? And what had happened to her?

The situation was bizarre and he wondered and hoped she was okay. He got up to make a phone call. Writing was a solitary and lonely undertaking and he needed to talk or even better meet with someone and connect if only for a few minutes. This was also part of his writing process, to stop after a good spell of writing, particularly when he was in the creative zone, as that meant he had something to return to whilst giving his brain time to soak up the subconscious links to his imagination.

He decides to call his neighbour who also worked from home running his own IT business. This involved fixing computers and laptops and also creating web pages for a small fee. They had both helped each other out. A trade by barter transaction and they would often meet for coffee to have a natter and give each other a break from solitude. This time he had something interesting to share and found himself getting excited as he dialled the number.

'Hi Scott, its Giles.'

'Hey, how you doing buddy?'

'I'm fine thank you, how are you?'

'Yea all good, can't complain. How about you? How's the writing going?'

'Yea, yea writing is going okay thank you. Always better when you have the crux of the story in your mind. Was wondering if you fancied meeting for coffee?'

'Ah really sorry, just waiting on a customer to pick up his laptop and I have to explain a few things. How about tomorrow?'

'Oh okay, yes its fine – tomorrow will be okay too.'

'Cool. I'll text you. I'll be free from four onwards. Have a good evening.'

'Okay great, you have a good evening too. Bye.'

Giles hangs up the phone a little disappointed as he may not be meeting anyone this evening. He saunters into the kitchen from the living room and pours himself a glass of water. He drinks the water in one gulp and places the glass in the sink mindfully. He's been trying to remember to do things with an alert mind so he is present in every moment. Especially when things had not gone his way, like him hoping to meet Scott for a chat and being turned down. He had never realised how hard this was. He was grateful for being a writer because the amount of time he spent in his head without an outlet, his head could quite easily have imploded.

He goes back into the living room and figures he might as well do some more writing but this time he was going to sit on the sofa. So he goes up the stairs to retrieve his laptop, comes back downstairs and sits on the end of the sofa. He gets back up and fluffs the pillow he is sitting on and then sits back down. He starts to type then stops. He thinks he can hear something outside and realises rain has started to fall. He smiles as he continues to type as this means he would not have to water the garden this evening. He is also not as disappointed now with not meeting Scott as it would have surely meant getting drenched.

As he types and is in a flow, he suddenly thinks about Paula again. What she said before leaving really bugged him. What did she mean by what she said? He stopped writing. He attempted to still his mind and he pulls the memory of Paula as she was leaving the house.

'The mind is a funny thing, it's also a beautiful thing, we don't quite fathom it, we don't even know how to use it, but one day we will.'

He shakes his head as if to throw the thought out and he carries on typing again but he's unable to stop thinking about Paula. The rain is falling hard now and creates rhythmic sounds from all the places around the house where the raindrops are making impact, big corners and small corners. It's like an orchestra of rain drops. He turns to the window and stares into space for a few seconds.

He then returns his attention to his laptop and saves what he has written so far. He has been typing now for over five hours. He is writing about a man's survival from abuse. Far too many books existed about women being abused; he thought, time to turn the cards. Men did suffer abuse from their spouses too and he was determined to create a compelling realistic story about it. Something compelling enough to perhaps explain why men would not ever report it due to the immense shame coupled with male pride. He scrolls up to the first page and contemplates the title he has given the book. "Derision."

This will do for now but he might change the title after completing the book. He found the right word often came after he had finished the book. The name popped out at you from the laptop so to speak and he would know without any doubt in his mind that the title was the right one. He often sought or preferred one word titles. He believed single worded titles were catchier and were more of a challenge to find, especially ones which encapsulated the story.

He turns the laptop off and gets up off the sofa. He checks the time and turns the radio on. He finds the radio calms him before bed, typically the classic FM station. He goes through his normal evening ad hoc routine of putting things off and pulling the blinds and checking the doors are locked. As he does so he smiles, wondering if everyone who lives alone goes through a similar routine. Could different routines or lack of, define someone's character perhaps? He would never have analysed something like this before he embarked on writing. Becoming a writer had made him more curious and had induced in him the ability to observe, everything about everything, which ideally helped him be present to each moment.

3

'Like everything, there are pros and cons.' Giles claims.

'Indeed.' Scott concedes.

'The place you suggested was awesome.' Giles proclaims.

'Yea it was pretty good huh – food, service and atmosphere, not normally you get all three together.' Scott agrees with a smile.

'Yep, even the capacity was right, not overly packed, like some established restaurants can be.'

'Good observation.' Scott nods his head smiling.

Both men walk in silence for a time. There is no awkwardness in the quiet. They saunter along the road in their estate with a confidence to their every step, a confidence honed from their familiarity with the estate where they've both lived for a number of years.

'Is work going okay?' Scott probes, suddenly breaking the silence.

'Yea can't complain, no matter what the day brings, I always think I'd rather be working for myself than stuck in an office or working for someone else.'

'Couldn't agree more – we're the lucky ones.'

'I don't believe luck has anything to do with it – we created what we wanted and we got it.'

'You truly believe that?'

'Yes I do – wholeheartedly. We create our universe every moment of every day. Yes shit happens, no disputing that, but even if the shit is runny we can still choose to close our mouth and eyes so the shit doesn't get into our very being and we can either sit out in the sun patiently, waiting for the shit to dry and then brush it off or we can immediately wash it off with water – we always have a choice.'

'Friggin hell, you do have a way with words.'

'I guess lucky for me I'm a writer.'

Both men laugh as they pootle up Claydon Street which they both reside on albeit at different ends. Giles lives at number 15 and Scott lives at number 65. They approach 15 first and Giles' attention is taken by a teenager standing on his porch. He's dressed shabbily and has unkempt hair. 'Now who could that be?' Giles mutters in a softer tone.

Scott stares ahead then returns his gaze back at Giles but doesn't say anything.

'Well, thank you again Scott, I'm not free for the next couple of days but perhaps do this again at the end of the week?'

'Sure that will be lovely.' Scott pats Giles on the back and continues walking up the street.

Giles approaches his drive, waiting till he's in hearing distance. 'Can I help you?'

The teen turns around to face Giles and smiles.

'Yes, I'm hoping that you can.'

The man is wearing a green long sleeved shirt and khaki trousers and on his feet he has sandals. They're the bulky pair, like jeep for feet. He has a broad face and a petite nose which sits pristinely over his exaggerated philtrum. He has plump lips and a dimple on his chin which is placed exactly below his philtrum.

Giles gets up to the porch having weighed the stranger up and down. The man steps away from the door allowing Giles to get to his door. Giles turns around whilst at the front of his door.

'Yes, how can I help?'

'Well, I think my cat may have gotten into your house. He has this habit of getting in through people's windows and I noticed the window at the back of your house, above the water butt was open.'

'Oh.' Giles glances round the front of his house.

'Yes, I'm ever so sorry to bother you. My name is Darren by the way and I live behind you on Crescent Street.' Darren puts out his hand to shake Giles; it's a firm handshake albeit with soft skin.

"Possibly a student." Giles thinks to himself.

'Well why don't we go in and have a look.' Giles says and opens the front door.

'Have you recently moved in?' Giles leads the way into his home.

'Err, yes, moved in with my mum a couple of weeks ago.'

'Well, welcome to the neighbourhood.'

'Thank you.' Darren says with a smile.

'Please...come in.' He drops his key on the sideboard next to the door and taps his broadband box till the connectivity sign shows – it doesn't flash and appears to be working fine.

'My broadband is playing up...So what's your cat's name?'

'Piper.'

'Okay, well feel free to call out.'

'Thanks...Piper!'

Giles is somewhat startled by how loud he shouted for his cat.

'Would you like something to drink?

'Yes, have you any juice?'

'Sure.' Giles saunters to the kitchen with slight apprehension as he waits for Darren to call out for Piper again. He wonders just how loud he will be this time.

'Piper!!'

Giles jolts at the fridge whilst getting cranberry juice.

"Yup...louder." He thinks to himself, smiling at how ridiculous he can be sometimes. He's always been frightened by sudden loud noises. He was certain he was on the autistic spectrum, and a bit off the average. However, he was informed not to refer to the condition as autistic spectrum anymore but Autism spectrum disorder (ASD), and some autistic people were irked when others assumed that because of one or two similar traits they were likely to be autistic. So he refrained from even mentioning autism. He never liked the idea of annoying anyone, not intentionally anyway.

Giles returns to the living room where Darren is standing looking out the window into the garden. He turns around to face Giles.

'Thanks...I guess the cat's not here.' Darren takes the glass and drinks some of the juice.

'I can go check upstairs if you want.' Giles starts to move towards the stairway.

'No...Please don't bother.'

'Oh...'

'There is no cat.'

Giles stops in his tracks and turns around abruptly.

'Wha – what do you mean?'

'I mean there is no cat and I'm not your neighbour and I'm not Darren.' The teen in shabby clothes now sits down and smiles looking up at a bewildered Giles.

'Then, what do you want?' Giles is now beginning to shake inside; there is something eerie about this young man, something he hadn't picked on before. He seems too at ease with himself, abnormally so. Also something in his eyes is familiar, he hasn't a clue why. The fact he had decided to sit down epitomises his portrayed quiet confidence and soft demeanour. This act thankfully softens the hold fear is having on Giles. He takes a deep breath and tries to calm his nerves.

'What do you want?'

'I need to tell you something...you have nothing to fear.'

'Why tell me a lie about a cat?'

'Because you would never have let me in and what I need to tell you would not have been conducive telling on the porch.'

Giles moves light footed towards an armchair adjacent to the sofa that the strange teen formerly known as Darren is sitting on.

'Please sit down.' The teen says with such calm, his voice could hypnotise the wildest animal.

Giles sits down, eyes fully focused on the young man who has coaxed his way into his home.

'What do you need to tell me?'

'Firstly you should know I'm not from these parts. I'm what some people would call a gypsy.'

"That would explain the clothing choice." Giles thinks to himself.

'There is someone you need to get hold of, someone in your past you weren't so nice to, your half brother who was introduced into your home. This time in your life was hard for you, a lot of abuse, it really wasn't your fault but neither was it your half siblings'.'

Giles is instantly taken back to his childhood when he lived in Nigeria. His mum had fallen in love with a black man who was studying in the UK. They started seeing each other and soon afterwards got married. His father later returned to Nigeria after his studies and not without taking his mum, him and his younger sister along.

All seemed fine in Nigeria for a short time anyway, until different women started coming to the house with grown up children, declaring his father was also their dad.

His mum was beside herself, she had given up her family in the UK to move to Nigeria with this man, who now turns out had impregnated various women before leaving to study in the UK. The situation was a complete mess and his mum was terribly sad and angry both in equal measure. She had lashed out when she could and his dad had hit back, beating her black and blue on many occasions.

In due course, his dad started sleeping out and over the years younger half siblings were introduced into the home. His mum had retreated into herself, and was like a shell of her former self. Giles and his sister were often left to fend for themselves, becoming malnourished, albeit not quite kwashiorkor* level but close. Both of them also exhibited poor personal hygiene as a result.

*A form of malnutrition caused by protein deficiency in the diet, typically affecting young children in the tropics.

One of the only things which had given him solace, despite escaping into numerous books and watching Lindsay Wagner as the bionic woman on telly, was the close relationship he had with a neighbour of his called Egbuke, who was a bit older than him.

Giles was only 14 years old at the time and his sister was a year younger. He could not help his mum and this did something to him internally. The fact he was powerless to protect his mum caused something sinister, dark and foreign to conjure up inside him. He thought to himself he may not be able to help his mum but he could sure do something to these so called half siblings being introduced and diminishing the perfect home they once had.

He picked on his six year old sibling - He would force feed him till he was sick and then make him eat his sick, till he vomited all over again. Giles took pleasure in doing this. The dark foreign entity which had consumed him, taking control of his faculties, was in full domination. The six year old would cry and beg for Giles to stop and Giles would finally leave him alone, but not before kicking him in the stomach and using his body to clean his sick off the floor. Another sibling he picked on was a year old and he would hold her nose till she couldn't breathe for a while and then let go. He would do this continuously, watching the little girl gasp repeatedly. And again he would take dark pleasure in doing this. They had come into their home and were destroying everything. They deserved to suffer.

'You remember.' The young man in shabby clothes stares sternly at Giles.

'Yes, yes I do.' Giles is now crying.

'Like I said, not your fault, you were being abused yourself.'

'What I did was unforgivable.' Giles cannot stop the tears.

'You don't know that until you ask.'

Giles is now crying uncontrollably. The teenager in shabby clothes gets up and moves over to him and embraces him. Giles sobs like a child into the stranger's shoulder. He shakes and sobs, holding onto the teenager as if he's known him for years. For a time he practically bellows, he is crying that loud. The floodgates have been opened, his shame has surfaced and he has nothing left to do but cry.

The young man in shabby clothes lets go of Giles and goes to get him a glass of water. He moves back to the armchair where Giles has sat down to wipe his eyes. He still blubbers like a child who has cried so long and hard he can hardly catch his breath. He takes the glass of water.

'Thank you.' Giles sniffs, he can't keep up with the amount of catarrh he's producing. He drinks the water in steady gulps. He is sure he has never cried so hard in his life. He's certain he's lost half his body weight in water through crying.

'I must go.' The young man announces.

'How...how did you know? How could you possibly have known this?'

'Does it matter?' The man peers down at Giles with a questioning comical face, his philtrum and dimple accentuate the look.

'I guess not.' Giles wipes his nose with his sleeve; there is so much snot on his sleeve, it's like the after party of a slug gathering happened on his garment.

'You know what you must do.'

'Yes. I am sure I can find them both on Facebook.' He had uninstalled Facebook from his phone many months ago as he found he was on the app way too much. But he had no qualms uploading it again.

'Good man.' The stranger pats him on the back as he makes his way to the door.

Giles promptly gets up.

'No, no please, I will make my own way out.'

'Won't you at least tell me your real name?'

'Bright.' He confesses smiling.

Why do Bright's eyes look so damn familiar? Giles can't help but ponder on this. Is it just because he feels so connected with him? He drops back into the armchair, he hasn't the energy to ponder where and how he remembers those eyes. He is as weak as used tissue paper. Tears still stream down his face as the stranger opens the door and strolls out into one of those distinct orangey dusks.

4

Giles is eating something light for lunch; he thinks this is apt as he's extremely at ease today. As if every molecule in his body got more space to fill and his lungs seem to have increased in capacity, allowing him to take in more air.

Reconciliation and redemption are the most powerful of human emotions. He had contacted his half brother who he had found via Facebook and they had talked until early hours of the morning. Whilst weeping, he apologised for the way he had treated him when he was little, affirming he had no excuse treating him the way he did. His half brother was now attending university and had a girlfriend. He listened at first and then thanked Giles, reminding him it was now all in the past. It was a terrible time for them all and he was not to blame himself. He didn't even blame their dad, not anymore anyway. He had made peace. Sometimes in life you had to muster all the strength in the world to let go. A challenge, that was a given, but he had managed to do it, through prayer and surrounding himself with positive people. He had managed to exorcise himself from his childhood. And he hoped Giles had done the same.

Giles thanked him for being so understanding and forgiving and said he was so sorry. His half brother told him to forgive himself. Giles cried some more. He told his half brother how he had attended a forum called Landmark Education* and how this had helped him exorcise his demons and the hold the wrath for his dad had on him. He had not been able to forgive their dad before as even though he knew he had to forgive for the sake of his own sanity, his mind and heart were not synced and so his forgiveness was never authentic.

*A personal and professional growth and development using Neuro-Linguistic Programming.

Only after Landmark Education was he able to let go. He had called his dad on the phone and cried buckets, forgiving him and thanking him for being the best father he could be. His dad choked on the other end of the phone too and he knew his act of forgiveness had instigated healing, healing long overdue. He had literally felt his heart move in his chest, making an audible cracking noise as the bloody muscle dislodged from some part of his ribcage. A blockage in his lungs was also melted away as he gasped in air. Until then it was as if he hadn't been breathing properly. The experience was the epitome of 'weight off your shoulders.' He had been carrying anger in his system for so long. Giles believed wholeheartedly, that it was these negative emotions that caused cancer, if not released from the body.

Soon after he had started meditating and he presumed this had had the same effect as praying which his half brother did. They later talked about happy memories, some existed, both he and his half brother found some. They spoke in Pidgin English and both laughed at each other. They shared about their present lives and what they had been up to and they both congratulated each other on how far and well they had achieved, considering their past experience. The connection they had on the phone was nothing short of magical. They were the moments you lived for. Moments of absolution you did not want to end, the only connected moments which encapsulated life so far as he was concerned. His half brother had forgiven him and allowed him to forgive himself.

Giles offered to send him some money to help him at university and his half brother was grateful.

Perhaps this was more redemption for him, either way he didn't care, he wanted to help and he was going to. He felt as light as a feather after he hung up the phone. 'Shame', it would appear, weighed a tonne.

Without too much hesitation he also called his half sister. She was newly married and was running her own business as a hairdresser. She couldn't remember having her nose pinched to stop her breath, as she was only a baby at the time.

She also listened attentively as Giles narrated what had happened and how sorry he was for doing that to her. This time he didn't cry, albeit he spoke with great centeredness and sincerity. Besides, he didn't think he had any more water left in him to shed. His half sister told Giles to be at peace, acknowledging they had a tough time. She remembered their dad doing a lot more terrible things to her than pinching her nose to hold her breath. She told Giles and he listened in part horror. She also told him she had forgiven him albeit they were not close; she had made peace and let it go. She told Giles after forgiving their dad, forgiving him for pinching her nose was nothing. It was the easiest thing in the world and Giles could hear the smile in her voice. This time a solo tear squeezed out of his right eye. Sometimes in life you have to muster all your strength in order to let go. "How had they been blessed with all this grace?" He thought to himself.

That evening he wrote freely about his experience of redemption not for any project he was presently working on, but he was sure one day, would be invaluable material for a book. He had two projects on the go at the moment and this is how he liked it, at least two books on the go. When he was stuck with one, he would work on the other and vice versa. When he was not writing he was happy to do research. He enjoyed the whole process; he received great joy when he was lost in imagination. He always thanked his mum for this. Had he not pined for her for years and years, when she left him and his sister in Nigeria, he didn't think he would have harnessed this ability so acutely.

Although his childhood experience had caused him great pain and still did, he was convinced the episode also gave him his writing skills, along with great empathy for others and an inner strength which seeped out of him at times of great adversity. So for this he was grateful and this was his healing too. To be grateful for his experience despite the pain, this he believed gave him grace.

As he sits in his study by the piano, he thinks about his mum and how much he had adored her. He had never loved anyone quite as much. Yet this adoration was somewhat unfounded, because his mum was not particularly mothering, at least not that he could remember. She was usually aloof and distant, granted this was exacerbated due to his father's violence and crassness but he couldn't remember any warmth from his mum when he was younger. He mostly put his love for his mum down to loyalty as the oldest son and his way of trying to reconcile that he was unable to protect her from his dad.

He picks up the picture of his mum, sister and him and stares at the image for what seems an eternity. He analyses the picture and wonders whether he saw sadness in the picture purely because of his state of mind over his mum or whether they were genuinely sad when the picture was taken. He wonders if it was his dad that had taken the picture. There was no one left in his family to ask, his mum was an only child. He puts the picture back down on the piano and decides to play a tune he was working on. As he played, he thought of the man who had come to see him, Bright, an apt name for someone who had come into his life momentarily and brightened it. He wondered how in the hell he knew about his past and thanked him profusely for creating the chance for him to seek redemption and a bit of peace. He also thought about Paula and wondered if she was okay. She said something profound about the mind as if she had listened to his thoughts just before ringing his bell. He could not remember ever having such an eventful, reviving week. He stops playing the piano and turns off the side lamp whilst getting up off the stool. The time was only 8:30pm but he decides to have an early night. He was exhausted from all the crying he had done.

He did the normal evening routine, which included brushing his teeth, getting into his pyjamas and climbing into bed and he thought about returning to the UK and how his mum had rejected him, out of fear of what her partner would think. That was so painful, but he didn't acknowledge the rejection at the time because his mum was dying of cancer. He smiled and turned the radio on. He didn't want to think of his past anymore. Enough was enough for one day. He closes his eyes and fills his mind with happy thoughts. He remembers swimming in the sea whilst on holiday in Crete with a good friend, playing Frisbee with another close friend and flying his kite and he reminisces over the many connections he had had with amazing people in his life, and still had. He was so lucky and appreciated his friends very much. He smiled some more as he stretched himself like a starfish in his double bed. In no time at all he was asleep, dreaming about his childhood.

 In the dream he was a superhero and he stopped his dad's punch from hitting his mum. He held his father's fist and crushed it in the palm of his hand. His dad's hands were big but that did not matter. He squeezed his dad's fist, crushing all the carpals and metacarpals till his dad's hand was mush. His father wailed in pain and Giles wailed in delight.

He then picked his dad up by the neck and threw him upwards out the house; his father smashed through the roof, catapulting across the night sky all the way back to Nigeria. In the dream, they all remained in Britain. He turned to his mum with a smile and said. 'Don't worry mum, he can't hurt you anymore.'

5

The next morning Giles wakes up early, it's still dark outside and he figures the time would be around 5am. He stretches in the bed having no idea about the dream he had had. He gets up and goes to the study and turns his computer on. He was going to make up for lost time through the last couple of days. He goes downstairs to put the kettle on. He always looked forward to his first cup of coffee.

As he walks downstairs he remembers he'd left his mobile phone upstairs. He wants to check to see if he had any messages, as he had retired to bed early last night. He gets to his bedroom, picks up the phone and checks; there was one message from his best friend asking him how he was and if he fancied meeting up next weekend. He smiles and takes the phone downstairs, replying to the message as he does so. He can see the Wi-Fi connectivity is almost zero. He checks the router and taps the black box gently. Nothing changes. He takes out the cable from the router box and leaves it on the side and walks into the kitchen to put the kettle on. He half fills the kettle; he prefers making a large full cafetiere of coffee so he could reheat more in the microwave if he needed, even for the next day. He wasn't fussed about the freshness. He got his caffeine kick no matter how fresh the coffee was.

He switches the kettle on and returns to the sideboard and puts the connecting cable back into the router and waits for a connection. He had read somewhere that the cable was an RJ11 and it went into an RJ45 socket but he didn't care about the minute details, although he was learning to be more and more detail oriented since starting a writing career. He thought of this as an analogy. If we could not be bothered about the details when someone spoke to us, then why be upset when we didn't have a fulfilling connection with someone. He recalls all the people in his life who took the time to enquire about the details when he was telling them something. He feels a keen sense of gratitude for this attention.

As he stands patiently waiting for the router to connect, a light tap on the front door startles him. This greatly unnerved Giles, even though the knock wasn't loud. 5:40 in the morning, who could be at his door at this time of the morning he wondered. There was a light tap again. It was as if the person behind the door knew he was standing on the other side. Giles looks through the spy hole and for a brief second could not see anyone but then spots a man who appears Middle Eastern. He seems distraught and looks like he has a bit of soot on his cheek. Giles is unnerved and slightly anxious. He wasn't sure what to do; it was so early in the morning. He then realises he was being judgemental and stereotyping because the man looked Middle Eastern. He had always promised himself he would combat this irrational behaviour. Making judgements based on someone's ethnicity. Amazing what the continuous bombardment of images from news headlines caused to the human psyche. He looks through the spy hole one more time, the man does look rather distraught and from what he can tell he seemed sincere. He takes a deep breath and opens the door.

'Please help me.' The man starts to cry.

'What's the matter?' Giles realises he was still being hesitant and irrational.

'Please come in.' Giles opens the door wider to let the man enter.

The man ambles in still crying and stands next to the sofa.

'Please sit down.' Giles scans him up and down looking for any muck on his clothes as the man sits down on the sofa. "Seems harmless enough," Giles thinks to himself and relaxes.

'Would you like something to drink?'

'Some water please, thank you sir.' The man requests with an accent.

'No problem, my name is Giles by the way.' Giles goes to the kitchen to get a glass of water. Being called sir always made him feel uneasy, possibly stemming from the white supremacy bull shit, even though he was mixed race. No one was superior over another and no one should be made to feel less than or more than anyone else. Christ, we were all in this together. Life was hard enough as it was without putting people into classes. Giles was instantly inclined to be extra kind to this man who appeared to be in his late thirties, was about 5ft 10in with a toned build. He had an unshaven face and deep kind mysterious dark brown eyes.

'What's your name?' Giles hands the man a glass of water.

The man takes the glass of water and gulps it down in one go. He wipes his mouth and takes a breath.

'Habib, my name is Habib.'

'Well, lovely to meet you Habib. Would you like another glass?' Giles smiles as broadly as he can muster.

'No, I'm okay - thank you.'

Giles sits down on the armchair facing the sofa and regards Habib.

'I'm so sorry for coming to your house at this early time sir.'

'Hey I was up anyway, and please stop calling me sir, Giles is fine.' Giles smiles with all his heart.

'Okay, thanks Giles.' The man starts to cry again.

Giles gets some tissue from the drawer nearby and hands it to Habib. Habib takes the tissue paper and blows his nose, then folds the paper one way and wipes his eyes. Giles hands him more tissue.

'Thank you for kindness...Giles.' Habib takes a deep breath to calm down.

'Well, you seem like a man in a lot of distress, I would be a monster not to be kind.'

'Some people don't open door.' Habib proclaims wiping his eyes. 'Thank you for opening door.'

'That's okay; just don't tell me you lost a cat.' Giles utters smiling.

'What?' Habib says with a quizzical expression.

'Oh nothing, someone came round the other day looking for his cat...Don't worry.' Giles realises that Habib whilst speaking in an accent appeared to have the British sense of humour and as if to confirm this Habib peeks at him and attempts a smile through a tear stricken face.

'What happened Habib?'

Habib turns away from the eye contact Giles is making and peeks out the window. He wipes his eyes again as tears roll out intermittently.

'My small sister got killed.'

Habib takes a deep breath and peers back at Giles.

'I'm so sorry.' Giles musters all the empathy from his being and puts it into these three words.

'She died in school; she was so bright, always wanted to learn, so unfair.' Habib wipes his eyes again.

'So, so sorry.' Giles sympathizes again.

'She was only eight.'

Giles empathises with the man's anguish. His compassion has increased following his redemption over his half brother and sister. He doesn't remember allowing himself to be this connected. He was often detached emotionally from someone showing emotion. It would appear that unleashing your hidden emotion allowed you to connect easily with other people's emotions, allowing others to open up even more. Made sense really, it was like the contagious act of puking or yawning.

'You're a writer yes?' Habib slowly lifts his head up from the rug he'd been transfixed on.

'Yes, yes I am but how did…'

'You have to write about it.'

'About what? How did you know I was a writer? Have you read something of mine?'

'Yes, I read the story about the Afghanistan textile designer.'

'Oh, okay...and you want me to write about something?' Giles tries to mimic the quizzical look Habib had given him earlier.

'Yes, people need to hear about other side of terrorism.'

'Oh...What d'ya mean?'

'No empathy and understanding on other side; never okay blowing people up, never, but deep understanding needed, people not realise their part and I think you may show them, enter the hearts of people on both sides of fence. Even more the extremist groups themselves. They are blinded by hate. Hate has engulfed them for reasons even they not sure.'

'Terrorism is physical violence but no one acknowledge passive violence which we have. Physical violence only come from victim of years of passive violence. Road rage, emotional abuse, conceited sarcasm, the hidden remarks we use on our loved ones sometimes, our pollution of the earth which we live on and even more dire our willingness to stay in this space by soaking in our various forms of addictive behaviours. No one wants to see this, no one wants to look at this deep, because it would mean that people have to take responsibility and you know what, people find it extremely hard to take responsibility.'

'This plus not listen properly to one another. Take a lot of strength and calm to listen and take full ownership for your life. People would much rather blame others, their parents, their colonists, immigrants, and their religion, anything but themselves. Because to acknowledge problem in self means to take full ownership and people no want, because think they not strong enough, which not true.'

'What happen to government after bombing middle-east for years? Weapon of mass destruction they say, but no weapon of mass destruction. What happen to government after this? Nothing. People choose their government. People all responsible.'

'Lucky, meditation and mindness become popular. People take more responsibility with more meditation. Spiritual revolution come. No one come into this world with too much they can't bear. In esoteric plane, this exist by the way.' Habib gives Giles another one of his quizzical expressions.

'We all choose exactly we want as challenge before come into world. Some take big, great challenge at the time. Chose all type experiences, understand deep that after challenge, true self come before God. God need to experience through us. This is how we must live. Lean into suffering, always present to it, make joke, laugh, love and speak true word all the time.'

'People have been writing and pointing out the truth for ages, it hasn't made much of a difference. What makes you think my writing will?' Giles asks calmly.

'Not true, people make difference; just take time is all. Peoples take their time. People have to be ready. Consciousness has to grow then change happen. It takes time, but in end it happen and everything people do, months and years, all enter consciousness of society. Slow progress, that's how it is with peoples. But no sad, never question, positive thing you do, it make difference. Never lost. Universe soak up and store, ready to pour into all consciousness when time right.'

'Wow that is a lovely insight.' Giles is momentarily aware of how present he is to Habib, as if he's been a pal with the man for years, eons even. Hard to believe he's only just met him a few minutes ago.

'You know what I say true.' Habib says and scans Giles with eyes that are less quizzical this time, but more celestial and pervading.

Giles smiles at the man but does not say anything.

'You no like match with others, you play devil advocate, like argue, analyse more, check and check. But you find not able to do this with me. This make me happy.'

Habib gives Giles a wide smile but this time with such sincere kindness in his eyes, it leaves Giles filling up with love and peace, like he has never before experienced. He tries not to fight this tenderness, instead allows the state to overwhelm him. He remains quiet and considers Habib, attempting to mimic the kindness in his eyes.

The entire living and kitchen space has been filled with eudaimonic happiness in an instant. Although eudaimonic happiness is something attained over time, Habib has somehow managed to attain this space in minutes. Giles has always had an inkling when it came to hedonistic pleasures. He has always believed that hedonism is short lived and hardly fulfilling. He has been aware of this all his life but never knew how to move away and instead go down the road of eudaimonism.

Later in life he started meditating and taking it seriously and started to be at ease and at peace with himself. He still partook in hedonistic pleasures, masturbating for one, but he had an unattached understanding of it now and always had his eudaimonic backdrop to fall back on to.

'Where are you from?'

'Well, not from this place.' Habib answers still smiling.

'I heard you saying that as I asked the question.'

'Where you from?' Habib maintains eye contact.

'Originally born in Cambridge, my mum and dad met when they were both at the University of Cambridge.'

'Intellectual type.' Habib continues to smile.

'What do you mean?' Giles smiles coyly.

'Nothing, mean nothing by it, except clear how much hard work you put for getting peace. Reality no come through intellect. Take something to have intellect brain drop intellect and surrender to nothingness, in nothingness you find peace.'

Giles understands fully what Habib is explaining. Ever since embarking on meditation, he knows being with your breath and sensing your surrounding somehow instils nothingness where peace resides. The 'meaning brain' is put to rest effectively and a space of emptiness which encompasses peace is created. This space is where true intent listening can operate in. This concept is also backed up in a very clear cut way by quantum physics.

'How exactly did your little sister die in the school Habib?' Giles exercises caution in his voice. He is not sure if he is being inappropriate by asking this question.

'A wall fell on her.'

'A wall!?'

'Yes school wall, a huge bang and light and then the wall give way and fall around and on top of her.'

'What could have caused that?'

Habib focuses on Giles, this time with a look of resignation.

'That's what I'd like you to write about.'

'Oh...okay, well I still need to know what happened in detail to ascertain and get a full story.'

'All in time, sense come when you ready and you will write when ready.'

'Okay...I hear you.' Giles fidgets a little in his seat.

'You process world auditory digital.'

'What?' Giles says finally attaining a more comfortable sitting position.

'Oh read later, must leave now. Promise me when time come you write about terrorism in true way, true way penetrate heart. Too much ignorance about it.'

Giles gazes at Habib square in the face. He embraces the restorative power that this stranger has instilled in him and knowing how rare it was to feel this kind of connection and how much he adored connecting with people on this level. He replies.

'I promise.' Giles does not blink.

'Thank you, now must go.'

'Okay.' Giles gets up and extends his hand for a shake.

'You know our big problem in world...Separateness. People believe no emotional strength to connect to everyone and everything, this lie; we ARE connect to everyone and everything, natural. Deny natural connection, we reduce, shrink, no living, like zombie.'

'I hear what you're saying but it is hard though, to stay connected and not be drained by it at the same time.' Giles spits the words out.

'Because to feel true connect also must disconnect.'

'That sounds like a contradiction.' Giles remarks again swiftly.

'Beautiful paradox of life – to live we must be okay with death, to connect we must be detached, to love we must be happy to let go too. Peace come from chaos and on and on.'

Habib gets up and pulls Giles towards him and both men embrace. Habib holds Giles firmly and whispers something in his ear. Both men release each other from their embrace at the same time.

'Thank you for all the insight.'

'You're welcome – thanks for making me welcome to your home and for not letting fear stop kindness.' Habib winks at Giles and Giles smiles even more broadly.

Habib moves over to the door and stands to the side so that Giles can open the door. Giles reaches to open the door and notes the internet connectivity on his router is unstable. He taps the router a couple of times but the interface box continues flashing.

'Thanks again. I know you write something true and everyone read.'

'I will do my very best.' Giles finally takes his attention away from the router.

Habib loiters out into a sombre late morning light. Everything that can be swayed is still from the lack of breeze and the light is polarised by the low temperature. A blanket of cloud spans across the sky, thin enough to let some light through and there isn't much sound from wildlife. One of those autumn mornings that can only be described as nature meditating, as if the birds know that their environment is meditating and remain silent in respect.

'Go well.' Giles has no idea where those words came from. He doesn't think he has ever used those words before to bid someone farewell. Why didn't he just say farewell – then again even that would have been alien in his vocabulary. Goodbye would normally be his chosen word.

'Thanks.' Habib turns left to walk down the road. He stops and turns back around.

'Watch for man called Tyler Conway, must act quick when hear or see this man.' Habib turns back around and starts to walk down the road again.

Giles stands and stares at him for a while. Wondering what on earth he meant by that. He makes a mental note but does not allow what he has said to destroy the reverence he has with him. He wishes him well and praises himself for not allowing fear to intervene with his truer self and basically common sense. He steps back into the house and to his surprise the connectivity on the router is on full again. He stares at the black box for a while as if trying to get some telepathic message as to what is going on with it. But of course nothing came. Routers have not advanced that much yet to give an electronic telepathic diagnosis of a problem.

He toddles back into the living room and gets himself a drink of water and peers out the kitchen window. The sky is orangey and cloudy; he smiles at the sombre weather. He likes the climate like this; it reminds him of the Harmattan* season in Africa. He's not too sure if it's largely the feelings it conjures up as it reminds him of specific events when he was a child growing up.

*A very dry, dusty easterly or north-easterly wind on the West African coast, occurring from December to February.

One particular memory was when he used to go to college during the holidays to study with a loyal friend of his called Karibo. They would study for a while and then go back to the dormitory where they would siesta together on a single bed, unavoidably touching bodies, both their hearts racing, both knowing they could hear each other's bloody muscle beating faster in their chests. They would do this every Saturday, both studying hard for about three hours in the morning in a deserted classroom, and then going for a siesta together.

Each summer they picked the same classroom. An overgrown bush grew by the window which attracted a lot of crickets. Subconsciously Giles was certain that they both picked this particular classroom to study in because of the rhythmical soothing sound of the crickets. Even though crickets on the whole chirped at night, at this particular classroom it seemed the non nocturnal ones gathered. The stridulating must have helped their learning brain process information. Giles remembered reading somewhere that you could tell the weather temperature by counting the number of cricket chirps in 14 seconds and then adding 40 which gave you the temperature in Fahrenheit. He later read somewhere else that this phenomenon referred to as Dolbear's Law was inaccurate as the study was done using the Snow Tree Cricket. The African field cricket, it would appear, was hornier and had an increased libido and tended to chirp when mating.

Giles would be lost in his studies for at least two hours but after that anticipation would arise from the thought of them going back to the dormitory to lie together to have an afternoon nap. This prolepsis would cause his heart to race and butterflies to flutter in his stomach and he always wondered if Karibo felt the same. One day this question was answered when as they both lay down, Giles facing away from Karibo. Giles felt a slight touch on his upper arm, at first he wasn't sure if an insect was on his arm and was about to smack his right shoulder with his left hand. Then he realised Karibo was caressing his upper arm with his finger. The touch was so tender that Giles felt himself relax even though his heart was still pounding in his chest. Eventually, Giles picked up the courage to turn around to face Karibo and Karibo planted a kiss on Giles's lips. They looked into each other's eyes and started to kiss passionately like it was the most natural thing in the world. And IT WAS the most natural thing in the world! Giles had later found out on various wildlife channels that animals also had same sex attractions.

About twenty years later, Giles had found out that Karibo was married to a beautiful woman and had two lovely kids together. Giles was predominantly attracted to men although he had enjoyed sex with women too and he could not help but wonder if the taboo with homosexuality in Nigeria had pushed Karibo to be with a woman and if he would indeed be a gay man if he was somewhere else in the world. Giles resigned himself to the possible fact he may never know and just wished and hoped that Karibo was happy.

This was a loving memory, one of tenderness and an innocence that was precious. Giles and Karibo had never done anything more than kiss. Although they could both feel each other's erection when they kissed, they both restrained from going to their groins, taking pleasure purely from the passionate kiss which got better and better over the summer.

Once, Karibo's parents nearly caught them as they were in full embrace in their living room, both Giles and Karibo pretended to be wrestling on the carpet. Karibo's parents stood for a few moments clutching their shopping bags and looking at them and eventually they smiled and carried on with getting the shopping bags emptied.

A few years later when they were both enrolled into the same University, Karibo happened to be in Giles' dormitory. He was visiting another friend. They ended up alone in the room. Karibo was on the bottom bunk bed and Giles on the top. Giles shimmied over and looked down after a period of uncomfortable silence and noticed that Karibo had his penis out and it was hard. Giles admired his vein riddled phallus for a few seconds, mostly because Karibo could not see him due to his positioning on the bed.

He eventually rolled back into bed lying as quietly as he could and for some reason chose not to do anything, even though he knew with all his quivering fast paced beating heart that Karibo wanted him to make a move. He didn't and so nothing happened. Giles would never know why he didn't make a move. He guessed it was because he wanted the magic of only the kissing to remain. Perhaps he didn't want the memory tainted by sucking dick!

Giles smiles as he reminisces. This memory was certainly an important anchor when stressed out or in an uncomfortable situation. There was no wonder that the environmental conditions reminded him straight away of the memory. The mind was a wonderful thing indeed. He remembers what Paula had said to him - 'The mind is a funny thing, it's also a beautiful thing, we don't quite fathom it, we don't even know how to use it, but one day we will.'

Giles smiles some more, what a bizarrely amazing week he seemed to be having. He checks the time and is amazed that it's 11:45 am. How quickly the morning has gone. Then again he is not surprised, time often moved speedily when having fun.

He feels the need to do some writing and he is famished and has body odour. He deliberates over which he should do first eat or shower and then mid thought, he grabs a pot, half fills the aluminium utensil with water, gently places two eggs in along with a timer that changes colour along markers which signify the eggs being soft, medium to hard. He puts the flame on and rushes up the stairs hoping that he will be able to have a shower in just over two minutes when the eggs should be perfect. He gets to his bedroom, peels off his clothes and throws them in the laundry hamper and then moves spritely towards the bathroom. He puts the shower on and waits for the temperature to be right and then for some reason, purposely hops in to the bath, making doubly sure he has enough room for his head and legs, so he doesn't accidentally hit them. Pleased with his agility, he puts the shower on and lets the sprayed water run over his body. There is something so relaxing about having warm water run over you. He cherishes the hot water droplets beating his shoulders and back for a while and then washes his armpits; he always did this part of his body first. Eventually, he starts to wash his privates, as he does so, he realises he's feeling horny.

"Masturbating will have to wait." He thinks to himself. "Having hard boiled eggs due to wanking was just not worth it."

He lets the water run over him some more, he purposely does not lather all his body. His dad had taught him from an early age not to lather his entire body all the time, as the skin became dry; he had always adhered to this advice, even when he had hated his father's guts. Who knew that this advice would one day come in handy when he could shower mega fast so as to get the perfect boiled eggs?

He stops the shower and pulls the towel from the radiator. He dries himself and puts the towel back. He grabs his bathrobe from the back of the bathroom door, and hops down the stairs whilst putting the robe on. He certainly has a bounce in his step and he is certain it is to do with the visit from Habib.

He arrives in the kitchen and takes the pan of boiling water with eggs off the heat. He has faith the eggs will be okay. He does not want to check the timer. But in the corner of his eye he can see that it is a little over the time for soft perfection. He pours the water out of the pan to stop the eggs from cooking further. He gets an egg cup out of the cupboard and places it on a small plate. He places one egg in the egg cup and the other on the side of the plate. He gets a small spoon from the drawer and gently taps the top of the egg. He then brakes into the shell and scoops the top of the egg with the spoon. The softness is still there albeit slightly over. "Not bad at all." He thinks to himself as he sits down on a side stool to enjoy his eggs. He puts a bit of salt and pepper to taste and digs in. He is mindful to be mindful about eating the eggs. He tastes the pepper and the salt which has an earthiness which complements the soft albumin protein. He questions whether this approach to mindfulness was okay. "It will have to suffice. I have a strong internal dialogue referred to as auditory digital in the NLP world and I am learning to live with this condition, in a kinder way so as not to beat myself up, all to do with learning to love myself." He smiles to himself as he allows this thought to engulf him and he gulps on another spoonful of egg.

The doorbell rings.

6

A storm is brewing, leaves and litter fly around a small park next to the estate that Giles resides on. The surface of a small lake nearby ripples continuously, due to persistent wind. Ducks on the water hurdle close together under some bulrush by the side of the lake. The sky is darkened even though it is mid afternoon. The atmosphere resembles that from a horror movie – take your pick. People can be seen looking up at the sky and then scanning around to find somewhere for cover just in case. The heavens are about to open and what will come forth could be hail or rain or a mixture of both and the size of whatever came down would be the size of small pets! It is that type of weather. Around the corner from the small park, Giles can be seen through a single hung window in a restaurant. He scans outside at the commotion which is beginning to brew in synchrony with the storm. He often came to this restaurant to have lunch and write when he needed a change of environment to kick start his creative brain. He always sat by the window if he could as he enjoyed watching people walk by and go about their business. He also enjoyed watching the lake and always thought the bulrushes looked like skewers with small rodents spiked on them.

He is fully present to his observation and this is when his creative mind is often unlocked, bringing something worthwhile to the forefront of his cerebrum. An explanation required in the book he was working on or an answer on how to kill a particular character off. He enjoyed planning someone's death whilst writing a book. He always picked on someone he hoped people had fully invested in emotionally and he would try to have their style of death be a metaphor on something he or she had been scared of. He was always delighted when he had a Eureka moment on how to kill someone and he was fairly sure he had a dark side that if exposed fully in a therapy session would possibly get him sectioned. Bulrushes seen as spikes with small rodents skewered on would certainly confirm this. At least he could play with this dark side of his safely in his writing.

Consequently, the heavens did open and hail and rain the size of small pets did come down. People scarpered for cover, some to their cars and some into shops. Quite a few piled into a Barnados charity shop across the road from the restaurant Giles was in. They all watched as the different forms of water came down, smacking the roads and pavements with such force, a back spray blur about five inches off the ground was created.

Giles watched solemnly, he does not remember the last time he had seen such a heavy downpour, not in Britain anyway. He recalls opening the door earlier to a passer-by just before he had decided to come to the restaurant.

The person that came to the door was an old lady looking for Wannermaker road. She was visiting her grandson who lived on that road. The taxi driver was lost and she had lost her patience and got out of the cab determined to ask and find the road herself. She was not prepared for the taxi faffing around and possibly charging her double or even quadruple for the ride.

Giles had checked on Google maps to help the lady as he empathised with her. Taxi drivers were getting worse with their sense of direction. You would have thought having above average geographical awareness was the prerequisite to being a taxi driver, apparently not anymore.

She was a lovely old lady, wearing a green cardigan over a pale yellow blouse and dark green trousers. She appeared trendy and Giles assumed she was at least middle class and from somewhere in south London judging from her accent. He had found the road she wanted, noting the name for future reference as it was a road close by to his street. He wrote directions down for her on a piece of paper which she thanked him for. As she walked off she folded and placed the piece of paper into her cardigan pocket but not before staring at the sheet for a while.

"Must have a good memory." Giles thought to himself. She was a sweet old lady and he always wished when he saw positive lively elderly people that he would end up the same way rather than bitter and cantankerous. He had informed friends before that if he ever turned out grumpy and bitter that they were to put him down immediately. They had assured him they would, as they would not want to be subjected to living the rest of their years with him like that either and they had laughed hysterically for a few minutes.

He remembers some years ago when he visited his grandmum in a care home. He visited her once or twice a week without fail. He had a great love for his grandmum as she had for all accounts suffered in life. She had only married once and her husband had had serious mental health issues and eventually had committed suicide from hanging. His mum was her only child and he had had to watch her go off with a man to Nigeria most probably fearing for her and hoping that she would be okay.

Her behaviour was cantankerous, negative and miserly and he understood she probably had every right to be, given the life she had had. Nonetheless, spending time with her was painful and he endured it for a few months before deciding to pick up the courage to tell her about her behaviour and how it made him feel. He was aware that in order to broach the subject, he would have to be extremely compassionate and the words would have to come from his heart. He was addressing the behaviour rather than her.

So one afternoon, after they had lunch together in the dining room with all the other retired people. He asked her if he could tell her something and they had retreated back to her room and he mustered all the strength in his being and told her how her behaviour made him feel. He said that he loved her and he wanted to see her and enjoy the time he had with her but that he wasn't enjoying the time and he was always checking his watch to when he could leave and he did not want to be like that with her. He spoke calmly and with great compassion, he was certain of this because he was not anxious and very grounded, as he shared his feelings with his grandmum.

After he was done, his grandmum gaped at him for what appeared an eternity; it was as if she had been hit in the face with a brick. Her actions after that for the next 3 months until she passed were just the most courageous. She completely changed her attitude and was more loving in every way. She hugged him warmly when he came and when he went and they had open and honest conversations, laughed out loud to stories they told one another and always enjoyed a game of scrabble and even once enjoyed a spliff out in the garden. It was if she had a new leash of life and they were completely present to each other. He never looked at his watch again after that and time just flew by. When she passed away, although he was sad, he took consolation in the amazing time they had as a result of his honesty and remained immensely proud of her for having the courage to change for him. He believed that what she had demonstrated was love in its purest form. She was eighty six and she had changed her behaviour because she was hurting someone she loved, her grandchild. They had set each other free from simply expressing a truth, wrapped up in love.

"All will become clear." That is what Habib had whispered to him before leaving. "Why had he whispered that?" Giles wondered. "He had said out loud, very loudly in fact, things that were a lot more profound – why whisper that? He guessed it was to ensure that he remembered it and if that was the case, then it was working perfectly."

He smiled and continued typing whilst noticing in his periphery vision that the rain was beginning to subside, such heavy downpour normally only lasted a short while. He typed away, allowing a sense of bliss and gratitude to flow as he did so. He was grateful for a lot of things in his life and he loved when he naturally got a sense of gratitude overwhelm him as he was aware that the universe gave more where there was gratitude. His smile beamed across his face and he continued to type. He was in the process of setting up the scene for someone getting killed. Again he wondered if his state of mind was healthy being that he was about to kill a character in his book whilst in a state of bliss. "It's just fantasy." He reconciled.

In his periphery vision he observed people starting to come out of their hideouts, albeit cautiously. Nature had the upper hand and this made him smile some more. "We are at the mercy of nature; it will do us good to be kind to the Earth." He thought to himself. He remembered Habib's comment on not despairing over positive actions that well intentioned people did in the world ever going in vain. A lot of people do amazing things in the world to combat all the greed and destruction that others do and the expression: (all will eventually come out in the wash), seemed an apt phrase to use after the heavy rain they just had.

Giles orders a cup of coffee and settles in to finish the chapter he was typing. He would do this and afterwards go home to prepare a light dinner as he had had something substantial for lunch. He would eat his dinner whilst listening to some soothing music to maintain the lovely mood he was in. He looks up out the window and the sun was coming out one last time before dusk. The atmosphere was always nice and fresh, the light was polarised and practically glistened the surfaces of most objects after rain. "There must be a rainbow somewhere." He thinks to himself. He soaks up the sensory experience for a couple more seconds and then tucks back into typing.

7

Giles wakes up with a muffled scream as his face was pressed into the pillow. He swiftly turns on his side and gasps relief as he puts his hands up to his head.

 He had dreamt that he was alone in a park and was having a picnic. He was waiting for someone but he didn't know who he was waiting for. He just knew that he was excited about meeting the person and looking forward to him turning up. He laid out the food items he had brought on a thick chequered blanket. Mostly he had nibbles that he had picked up from the local Aldi but he had brought with him a jar of courgette chutney that he had made the previous year. He had saved this for a noteworthy occasion and was happy to bring the jar to the park for this affair.

As he sat in bed thinking about the dream, he thanked the heavens that it was all a dream. He wondered if he may have been waiting to meet a date but he wasn't sure.

In the dream, he laid out all the food items. Salads and organic vine tomatoes, coleslaw, honey and lemon chicken pieces, pate with hard crusty bread, olives and sundried tomatoes and homemade sausages that he had left in the fridge the day before.

He felt something move in his ear. Since turning forty eight and getting his ears syringed because of a throbbing pain in his right ear a few months back, he had started experiencing the novelty of bits of ear wax dislodging from his ear on their own accord. Why nobody informed you about these things as you got older he would never know. Like the reserve wee that came out of you when you brushed your teeth after you had already urinated, seeping out uncontrollably so much so you were forced to brush your teeth over the toilet, learning a new balancing act of peeing and brushing at the same time. Or even more derailing, the conflict of younger self and older self fighting with who gets the upper hand – out for the night or stay in with Netflix?

There was a real struggle and an inevitable sadness that ensued because it was a stark reality of you aging. Does mid life crisis pan out the same for everyone? Or can this sense of time running out be spread out? How do you know when you are going through midlife crisis? Does everyone go through a midlife crisis? So long as he didn't end up cantankerous he would be okay with bits of himself falling out involuntarily. If he turned out grumpy and bitter he could just imagine his grandmum laughing hysterically from the other side.

He sits on the blanket arranging the food items; he grabs a paper napkin, folds it and uses it to pick at his ear. He picks what he thought was a ball of ear wax but when he brings the napkin to his line of vision is shocked to observe a maggot wiggling in the serviette. He briskly stands up and starts to dig at his ear more with the napkin. He continues to feel the wiggling sensation. More and more maggots fall out of his ear. They drop all over the display of food on the blanket. He begins to panic and drops the serviette, frantically clawing at his ear to expel these small disgusting wiggling creatures. Then he starts to get the same sensation in his other ear. That is when he wakes up.

'What the hell kind of dream was that?' He verbalizes out loud as he checks the time, only 5:45am. Another thing that happens when you reach 40, you start waking up really early, having a lie-in just didn't appeal anymore. Giles sits up in bed and thinks about the dream, so vivid. He still isn't sure who he was waiting for in the dream, but whoever it was, it was someone special.

He gets out of bed, drinks some water from a filled glass by his bedside and meanders to the bathroom. He needs to do a number two. He hoped it would be one of those satisfying defecations. The one you did where you felt everything had come out. You just know when you have cleared your bowels properly; your stomach is deflated, you feel light and cleansed and your day starts off just nicely.

Regular bowel movement became an exciting event as you got older, something you didn't care about when you were young. As Giles sits on the stool pushing, he senses instinctively it was going to be a satisfactory one as he feels it move from his deepest colon. He smiles as he pushes and immerses himself in the bowel movement which is causing a poogasm. He uses the experience to throw out the horrible nightmare he had had.

He reaches for toilet roll and wipes his bum several times. Checking the toilet paper each time after each wipe, he wondered if everyone did this. "How else would you know if you had cleaned properly if you didn't check?" He thinks to himself. He was happy he had gotten everything and still smiling he gets up and flushes the toilet. He watches as two faeces' swirl around and around, one large and one small. The larger one goes down at the precipice of the flush but alas the smaller one remains. Giles tuts to himself as he reaches for the hand soap and squirts some of it on his hands; he washes both hands under the tap as he waits for the cistern to fill up. "It was going to be one of those days." He thinks to himself. "When you have to flush more than once to get rid of your morning poo, it was going to be one of those days." He smiles and makes a decision to write it down as it would make for a nice entry in some book he wrote. Anything for people to relate to and hopefully make laugh, and most people he reckoned, would relate to shit.

He flushes the toilet again and watches as his poo swirls and twirls, resisting the pull to go under, Giles watches in anticipation and it seems that the second flush was not going to take the turd down either and then with one final swirl the turd was gone. Giles smiles, with a sense of victory. "It was the small things." He thinks to himself. "Well actually it wasn't that small, that was part of the problem." His smile broadens.

He has another memory of Nigeria. Once they travelled to Foropa, their dad's village, which was in a remote area on the delta. The toileting arrangements took some getting used to. There were wooden sheds held up over the river by stilts and a hole where you squatted to have a poo. There was a wooden door with a latch so you did have your privacy which was a plus. As soon as excrement dropped, strange creatures with bulging eyes called mudskippers would immediately emerge from the mud to feast on the faeces. In actual fact, they didn't emerge. They were the mud. They were perfectly camouflaged. And when the poo hit the mud all there bulging eyes would open at once. They were like very large tadpoles with fins on their back and they literally immersed themselves in the faeces which was quite entertaining to watch whilst having a number two. As the name suggests they skipped along the mud and would sit still on occasion just watching with their large bulging eyes. They were happy to conceal themselves from predators, at least until excrement hit the mud and then they felt it was worth the risk to jump on that poo. They should really have been called poo skippers. They were indeed comical, fascinating and disgusting creatures all one.

"I dare Walt Disney to make a film about the mudskippers of Foropa!" Giles thinks to himself.

On your visit to the loo, you were given a small jerry can of water which was used to wash your bottom once you were done. This also took some getting used to, but I remember thinking that this was certainly a better way to clean your behind after going for a number two, so long as you remembered to wash your hands afterwards...properly.

He stands and contemplates whether to have a shower whilst in the bathroom or go down stairs and make a cup of coffee first. He decides to go down and have a coffee. He grabs his bathrobe and wraps it round himself and goes down the stairs mindfully. He had gotten into the habit of doing this since meditating. Every time he used the stairs whether going up or down he would take his time, being with each step and feeling the carpet beneath his feet. It was a great way to be present.

As he reaches the front door he automatically looks at the router and this time the connectivity is on full. He turns around and walks into the kitchen and puts the kettle on to make his coffee. He was engrossed in the characters he was creating for his book and one in particular who had a multifaceted personality he was very fond and proud of. It was almost as if the character had a mild personality disorder.

He had once volunteered at a mental health care unit looking after the patients. He had only managed to carry on doing this for a couple of months before giving up. Even though he only worked twice a week he found it mentally exhausting. At the time he had not learnt to detach. Detachment he felt was a prerequisite if you were to care for people with mental health. He took his hat off to support staff (if he ever wore one) – This expression was only probably appropriate in the western television series. Probably a better expression would be "he saluted them," yea definitely, he saluted the people that worked in the care industry full stop.

They worked their socks off, were open to numerous allegations and got paid peanuts. He figured if things didn't change and fast, either with work conditions and or pay; a major crisis was going to erupt in the care industry which would cause safeguarding alerts to go off the charts. People ordinarily avoided the care industry like a plague – you only had to look at job vacancies.

At least 60% were always jobs as care or support workers. No experience required was often highlighted in bold. That is how desperate care providers were for staff. Until the due respect deserved was given and this reflected in the pay, there would remain a shortage in staff and hence a potential for safeguarding cases to rise. What irritated Giles more than anything was that some companies operated on what he called the 'scapegoat principle' where a member of staff driven to exhaustion from working inhuman hours and thus inevitably 'messing up' due to the extreme pressure, was held accountable and punished. No one tended to look at the system, the broken stretched tired system that pushed people to extreme behaviours. That would be too much hard work.

This red tape, bureaucratic bullshit was one of the reasons he had chosen to be an author and work for himself, he could only then be accountable for himself. Most managers had not worked on the ground and so had no idea. They hadn't the emotional intelligence and or the inner confidence to deal with people with strong personalities. They often didn't do much and just delegated without any consideration for the workload the staff were under.

Scott would certainly agree. Talking about Scott or thinking about Scott, he hadn't seen him for a while – he was going to call him and plan another meet. They were supposed to meet the following weekend but Scott had called to cancel.

He pours his coffee – He had boiled the kettle, put coffee in the cafetiere, poured hot water over it and waited for the coffee to brew all whilst he was lost in thought.

He sits down and takes a sip of his caffeine laced beverage. He delights in the fact that he never had to rush anywhere. He took his time in the mornings and this was owed to working on his own. He takes another sip of his coffee.

He decides to call Scott. He grabs his mobile phone which is on the table next to him. It was always next to him except when he was using it to play music from iTunes. It was safe to say he was a slave to his phone and he was certain so was everyone else these days.

He beckons to Siri to call Scott and taps the speaker button, the phone is immediately activated and a dialling tone initiated. He started always putting the phone on speaker as it broke up the silence in the house from living on his own.

'Hello.'

'Hello Scott, Giles here.'

'Hey Giles, so glad you called - I passed my exam.'

'Great news Scott...awesome news. We should celebrate.'

'Well, as it happens I'm organising a get together in the primary school. You should come.'

'I would love that very much – thanks for invite. I have an awful lot to tell you. After that guy that was at my door when we came back from the restaurant, the most bizarre group of people have dropped by.' Giles is aware this isn't entirely true.

'What guy are you talking about?'

'The guy in scraggly clothes that was at my front door.'

'I don't recall seeing a guy by your front door.'

'You didn't see the teenager that was at my front door when we returned from lunch?'

'No.'

'You're messing with me right?'

'Nope, definitely didn't see a teenager at your door.'

'Hmmmm okay, bizarre cause I'm sure I commented on it as you walked off.'

'I'm sure there's an explanation. Maybe I was distracted; studying for an exam will do that.'

'Okay, yeah I guess so. Okay see you later.'

'Yup, it's going to be fun. Bye bye for now.'

'Bye.'

Giles ends the call and looks perplexed. "How could he not have seen him? He was right on the front porch. He must be playing with me. He'll get to his celebration party and Scott will slap him on the back laughing out loudly that he had fallen for his prank. He wasn't sure he would find it at all funny."

"Okay...okay now what to wear. He hadn't been to a party in ages. Was there a kind of dress code for a celebratory event? Damn it, he should have asked. He was so taken aback by what Scott said it had completely derailed him and he had forgotten to ask the most important question. He thinks to text him, and then thinks, on this occasion, a straight man really wouldn't be able to help him.

"Hang on a second, the CCTV cameras, I can check the footage." Giles laughs to himself on two counts - thinking to ask Scott for advice on attire and not remembering that he had installed CCTV. He will not have time to sieve through the footage right now, it will take some time and he needs to figure out what to wear. He will check it when he returns from the party.

Giles sprints up the stairs and enters his bedroom. He stands by the window for a few moments looking out at the garden. He is jittery but can't put a finger on the strange foreboding that has engulfed him all of a sudden. He has battled with anxiety most of his life and he was managing it pretty well since meditating and attending gym. This was different though, some excitement was in the mix but he couldn't understand how and why he would have this sense of impending doom. He wasn't sure if the fact that he had been meditating for the last year was lessening the intensity of the feeling that he had or was exacerbating it. After all, meditation opened you up more – It brought clarity, and perhaps he was sensing something deeper and more disturbing than he had ever experienced before.

The dread he experienced reminded him of the time he believed he was having a nervous breakdown. The foreboding wasn't as intense, thank God, but Christ it was near enough. He was starting to get sweaty palms coupled with a racing heart. He sure as hell did not want to relive that experience he had a few years ago, before attending the Landmark Forum. He had finally synced his whole system into forgiving his dad authentically and the reward afterwards was heaven.

He had woken up one morning and genuinely felt like he was about to lose his marbles! It was like he was standing at the precipice between sanity and insanity and he had his leg hovering over the line. He just had to take one more step and he was going to be in the space of forever enduring lunacy, which would not only consume him but own his soul. It was an experience he never wanted to relive ever again. He wouldn't wish it on his worst enemy, if he had enemies. He had gotten clear so far. Why was he feeling like this? He can't be going back to this, surely not. He took deep breaths and put his hands onto the window pane and inhaled fresh air from the window into his being, wishing it to replace the stale air consisting of fear molecules that had somehow seeped into him.

He carried on breathing in deeper and deeper and expelling air from his mouth. He was determined not to beat himself up about this little set back. He remained positive. "I have made it up to now and damn good. This is just a glitch, nothing more. I'm shaken a little is all...It will make sense, it'll all be fine." He remembered what Paula and Habib had said to him.

Giles also remembered a couple of occasions when he worked in the care home for mental health and how one non verbal lady in particular used to sometimes be so sad. She would sit and stare out the window with such sadness in her eyes; it was as if she was carrying the sorrow of the world. It was only twice that he witnessed this but it was enough to entrench deep in to his being – It was so desperately sad to watch.

Most of the time the lady was quite eccentric and she would play pranks on people and run away and laugh hysterically. She was certainly a character and all the staff adored her, which made it difficult when she was having her blue days. He thought about this because in some way that is how he felt. He couldn't quite explain it but it was a deep sadness soaked up in anxiety and fear.

He used to think that some of the people at the mental institute were vessels, carrying the souls of several people in one body which caused an inner conflict that was almost unbearable and these people often turned to drugs for relief. This was a reincarnation theory he thought of for a long time, one he was all too aware was far-fetched but one he thought of as possible nonetheless. Since reading up on quantum physics he wasn't too quick to discard any kind of belief or theory.

Giles continues to breath and is more accepting; he closes his eyes and stays with the space he finds himself in, not allowing fear to overwhelm him. Eventually he starts to calm down; his heart rate starts to reduce. He turns around, but not before noticing his full hand prints on the window pane. It's as if he had been playing - pat a cake, pat a cake with the window. His ghostly handprints appear to stare back at him momentarily before leisurely vanishing. He turns around and strides over to the wardrobe. He opens the wardrobe doors and stares at the array of clothes before him. He wants to put on bright colours; he believes this will combat the temporary dark cloud that is over him.

'Phew.' Giles gasps as he starts to sieve through the clothes looking for the colour that will take his fancy. His decision not to text Scott is right, he will turn up smart but casual, you can never go wrong then.

8

Part of Giles has always liked the limelight; he has mastered the art of playing the clown which he had to develop to alleviate his anxiety when around crowds of people. He was able to do this with little effort, when he was in the right state of mind. Sometimes though he was also happy to sit in a corner and observe. He would often seek out the shy person that no one was talking to and he would home in on them and make pleasant conversation. Whilst he enjoyed the limelight he was not bothered if he was not in it. He often found people that were not part of a group more interesting and he enjoyed one to one chats more so than group gatherings.

This evening he was sitting down in the corner of the room and was observing for a bit, to take in the atmosphere. Scott had welcomed him in and stood chatting with him for a while and then had gone to mingle, asking Giles to do the same. A part of Giles always resisted a request like this – He rather took on social challenges like this on his own accord. So he decided to sit down and take it all in first, scanning the room of all the people and deciding which person to go up to. It was always a little unnerving but he continued putting himself in these situations when he could because he knew it was better to face your fears, whatever they were.

Eventually he spots a lady sat in the far corner of the room. Scott had decided to have the party in the primary school grounds which was on their estate. At weekends the school was open to the community for various events for a little price. They were large rooms with wooden floors and high ceilings and despite the size; the acoustics in the room was fine. In fact the acoustics was perfect for music and some low key disco parties organised for birthdays.

The lady that Giles had finally laid his weary eyes on was sat in a corner by a frosted sash window and she looked at everyone with a smile that remained serene for the time that Giles kept watching her. Occasionally she looked out the window admiring the school garden which was particularly impressive when lit up with soft coloured flood lighting. The lady was thin and sat with confidence and grace, taking the occasional sip of her wine which she kept on a shelf in her line of vision.

Giles detects a spare chair by the lady and wonders if she had deliberately sat there for this reason. He decides to go up and chat to her. He often found it less petrifying to speak to a lady and was certain that this was because he was gay. Speaking to a guy in these kinds of events was a whole different matter because he was attracted to guys and so there was presumed to be another agenda. He would often become typically nervous if the guy was attractive. With ladies there was no agenda at least not on his part. He often found that women soon relaxed when he gave away his sexuality.

He starts to walk towards the mysterious lady in the corner, who was confident enough to be sitting on her own in a social gathering. He is a few feet away when a man introduces himself to her, stopping Giles in his tracks. The man is wearing a tweed jacket and a jazzy pair of trousers and reminds Giles of illustrations of Rupert the bear. The lady retains her smile and as Giles is now within hearing distance he overhears the lady introduce herself. Her name is Flora which suited her elegance and the floral dress she was wearing which was a simple design and covered with purple and yellow tulips.

Giles, who is now standing by a slender bookcase pretending to admire an art piece created by a kid in year four; can see now that she is middle aged, possibly in her early 50's. She looks exceptional for her age; he was willing to bet that she was vegan judging by how slender she looked. He is abruptly snapped out of his conjecturing by a pat on his shoulder.

'Mingling with the bookcase I see.' Scott teases.

'Was admiring this piece of art actually.' Giles responds promptly whilst pointing to the art on the wall situated to the left of the bookcase.

'I see.' Scott responds before swigging from his bottle of beer.

'Come with me, I want to show you someone.' Scott pats Giles on his shoulder again.

Giles cannot help but return his glance to the lady in the corner. Something about her was now captivating, the way she speaks to the man who has introduced himself as Toby. She retains her smile but her eyes aren't smiling along. He is certain that he can see concern in her eyes. The man has sat himself down, pulling his chair that close to Flora their knees are almost touching, as if to ensure that no one else can hear him.

'Giles, you okay?' Scott interrupts.

'Yes, yes...do you know that man?' Giles queries whilst tilting his head in the direction of Flora and Toby.

Scott turns in the direction suggested. 'Yes, I believe he lives two roads down from us, keeps himself to himself though. Why?'

'And the woman?'

'What about her?'

'Do you know her?'

'I think she's new to the neighbourhood, I believe she's a clinical psychologist. She lives on her own and there are rumours that her son is in prison for rape.'

'Oh...that's unfortunate. How on earth did you find that out?' Giles keeps a corner eye on both Toby and Flora.

'Do you mind telling me what's going on? Why are you acting like a detective all of a sudden?'

'Well, I think that lady is being intimidated.' Giles turns away from both of them now as he catches sight of Toby looking up in his direction.

'What makes you say that?' Scott probes with slight concern in his voice.

'Well, they don't know each other but look how close the man is to her.'

'Okay...still not getting how that means she's being intimidated.'

'You don't immediately sit that close to someone you've just met, not unless there's something sinister going on and I'm willing to bet something sinister is going on. I think I'm going to walk right up to them and interrupt their...yea I'm going to do just that.'

Giles turns on his heels and paces towards the woman that has somehow captured his interest. He has an urge to help her from something; he just isn't sure what yet. Scott puts out his hand to tap or perhaps grab Giles' shoulder but he is too late.

'Hi.' Giles announces with the biggest charming smile he can muster.

Both Flora and Toby look up at the same time.

'I couldn't help but notice your tweed jacket; I've been looking for something like that for ages.'

Flora regards Toby who is now looking at his sleeves.

Giles smiles at Flora who returns the smile as he would have expected.

'What are you, some kind of queer?' Toby gets up to confront Giles.

'Hi.' Scott puffs up as he marches up to Flora, Toby and Giles.

Toby glimpses at Scott and back at Giles who does not say a word. Giles doesn't know how to respond to the question. He can't remember the last time he was faced with homophobia.

'I think perhaps you should apologise to this young man.' Flora suggests with unfounded confidence that appears to have sprung from nowhere.

Scott takes another calculated step towards Toby, looking at him sternly.

Toby regards both Scott and Giles and returns his attention to Flora.

'We will continue this later.' Toby turns to look again at Scott and Giles before walking bullishly away.

'You okay?' Giles finally gets his voice back.

'I should be asking you that. I'm totally fine, he's more bark than bite.'

'What was that all about?' Scott glances inquisitively at Flora and Giles.

'I shouldn't be disclosing this but he's overstepped the line. His wife, soon to be ex wife, is a client of mine.'

'Oh.' Giles utters.

'Client?' Scott interrogates, looking at Flora, pretending not to know about her profession.

'Yes, I'm a psychologist.'

'I see, and he's pissed off about how his wife is behaving after sessions with you?'

'Something like that, yes.' Flora says checking her phone.

'He's just scared, scared of what his life will mean when he has no one to intimidate or bully.' Flora puts her phone away.

'Thanks a lot for interrupting our chat though, I really appreciate it. Whilst I'm not scared of him myself I do worry, even more so now, about his wife. I think I'll have to take this to the police and may need your input. I think his wife may be in danger.'

'Sure, anything you need, the man seems like a real jerk.' Giles declares.

'He must have been watching me for some time to know that I was here.' Flora says whilst taking a notepad out and writing in it.

Scott regards his arranged social event momentarily then returns his attention to Flora and Giles.

'I'm going to make sure that arsehole leaves.' Scott claims and marches towards the exit.

'You sure you're okay?' Giles pulls the chair slightly away from Flora and sits down facing her.

'I'm not scared for me; I'm scared for his wife. I know I said he's more bark than bite but I think he has no hold on his fear at all and that's always a scary thing with people, especially ignorant people with poor reasoning potential. Egomaniac people like that guy have to have some sense of control in midst of their fear, otherwise they become very unpredictable and that's my worry. His name isn't Toby by the way, have no idea why he lied to me about his name. He must have known his wife would have given me his name. He's Mr Conway.'

'I'm glad you're okay.' Giles finds himself saying, still somewhat mesmerised by Flora's charisma that he hasn't noted the name that Flora has mentioned.

'Thanks, you're very sweet.' Flora smiles with both her mouth and eyes.

Giles exhales in relief, now seeing the same smile that he had witnessed when he first laid eyes on her. He has no idea why he is drawn to this woman but he is drawn towards her, strongly. The whole situation had stopped him obsessing over looking at the CCTV camera's when he got back home.

'You're a special kind of guy.' Flora examines Giles with sincere kindness in her eyes.

'Well thanks, whatever makes you say that?' Giles replies coyly.

'Saying what I see.'

'Thank you.'

'You're welcome; people don't often say what they see. I think the world would be a much better place if people said what they saw. Often people can't see for themselves, traits that are not helpful and people witness it and choose not to say anything out of some kind of misplaced kindness. I would rather someone tell me I was being a buffoon than not know, then again I would probably be out of work.'

'So far as the truth is pointed out with compassion then yes I agree wholeheartedly.' Giles remembers his grandmum and smiles.

Scott tootles back towards them.

'He's definitely left, can we now please enjoy the party.' Scott says.

'I'm sorry I was part of that debacle.' Flora gets up.

'Don't be silly, had nothing to do with you. He's possibly one of the most truculent of people I've met in a long time.' Scott says with a smile.

'I was going to introduce you to someone before we were rudely interrupted by the...Neanderthal man. Can I introduce you two to someone please?' Scott says.

'Certainly.' Flora joins the men and they all walk towards a gathering of people.

9

Giles cannot walk hurriedly enough towards his house. Whilst he was distracted for most of the evening due to the charisma of Flora – he had honed back in on his obsession with seeing the footage of the CCTV camera.

He gets to the door and takes a peak at the small camera which is camouflaged nicely in ivy creeping up a concrete pillar by the side of his house. He opens the door and for a moment it seems his hands are shaking, he stands and stares at his fingers for a while, he can't see any trembling, and realises it's all in his mind. He smiles and enters the house putting the keys down next to the router on the sideboard. He takes another quick glance at the router before moving on; it appears to be working properly.

He heads straight to the utility room which has the washing machine and a vanity cupboard where he stores most things of a discrete nature like condoms, lube and certain sex toys. It also has a built in desk and a chair as sometimes he chose to sit and write in there for a change of scenery and hopefully some boosted motivation. He believed a change in temperature helped with changing perspective and other creative pathways in the brain. He also believed the somewhat sterile nature of the utility room helped create a clearing in his mind when he needed it the most.

On the desk is a monitor connected to the CCTV and a computer screen. Giles sits down and for a moment stares at the desk space recollecting his thoughts on how to use it as he does not look at the footage often and can't remember the last time he did.

He pulls out a small drawer and switches a button and turns the computer screen around. He plugs a cable in the back and waits for his computer to boot up. He double clicks on the 'Super Net surveillance' icon on the desktop and clicks on the Login screen and waits a few seconds, his anticipation increasing.

He shuffles in the chair he is in and scans the utility room. The screen pings at him and he scans it, his heart racing. He remembers the screen and clicks on the date icon, as he does so he tries to remember the date the chap was stood at his door when he returned from lunch with Scott. He remembers the date and clicks on it. Then he clicks on the time, he guesses it was around 3pm and so he waits and watches. The screen fills up with a shot from his front door, showing the entire cul-de-sac. He starts to fast forward and carries on looking, still no one. He tries to remember if maybe it was around 2pm they came back and as he is about to click rewind, he spots in the distance both he and Scott walking towards the house. He moves closer to the screen as he is certain that the guy in tattered clothes will appear soon enough.

A car is seen stopping outside his house and a guy gets out of the car and Giles sits back in his chair thinking to himself he certainly didn't think the guy would have been dropped off. The guy scans the area then walks towards his neighbour's house. Giles pouts as he moves closer to the screen again. He can see Scott and himself approaching the house a few yards away and he is certain it is about the right time he spots the person at his doorstep but no one. Then the chap appears; as if he materialised from nowhere. He scans around and strolls up to the porch of Giles house.

He continues to watch and can now see Scott walking away and himself walking towards the house, towards Bright. Giles is disappointed but relieved at the same time. So Scott was just winding him up about not seeing him. He smiles a little and sits back in the chair staring at the monitor and fully witnesses himself approach his porch and enter into dialogue with the young man.

He decides to find the date when Paula showed up at his house. He finds it in no time at all and lets it roll. He sits and waits, expecting in no time at all for Paula to show up at the porch. He plays with his fingers as he watches. He has made a lot of effort to stop biting his nails and instead now he rubs his fingers together. He continues to watch, noticing a bird almost fly into the camera in search for ivy fruit. He can't make out what type of bird it is as it's overcast. He checks the time on the monitor and is sure it is about the time that Paula showed up. He doubts anyone could ever be prepared for what he then witnesses.

He freezes and gapes at the monitor as he witnesses himself open the front door. He is talking, but no one is there. He freezes the screen and wonders if he somehow clicked on the wrong date. He checks the date and he is sure it is correct. He rewinds the tape and continues to see the same, him at the porch talking to no one. Giles is now bewildered, he doesn't know what to make of what he is seeing or as it happens not seeing. He can just about make out the side of his face and he is looking ahead and talking. He watches himself talking to no one and he unexpectedly feels cold. His body has forgotten how to regulate his temperature. Giles gulps and recognises the signs of a possible panic attack. What exactly is going on here? He freezes the screen again and inspects closely. There is no one except him. He is the only one visible on the screen and talking to someone that isn't there. He sits back in his chair, his heart now racing. His brain is unable to make sense of what he is witnessing. He taps the monitor and then taps the computer screen, knowing deep down that this is factitious of him, but it's the only thing he can do to somehow check the reality he finds himself in. Is it possible to have a fault with the camera feed so much so that it does not pick up something? Is that possible? He's desperately trying to make sense of what he is observing in his utility room and he can't. He's unable to figure out any logical explanation to what is happening and starts to wonder if he's going mad. He pinches his forearm and closes his eyes tightly shut and then opens them again and what he perceives hasn't changed, him standing on the porch chatting to an invisible person that is not showing up on the screen. He saw and chatted with her a few days ago. Now he is embroiled and just as he is trying so hard not to have a panic attack. The doorbell goes. This makes him literally jump out of his seat. He places his hand on his heart and wonders if it could beat so fast it just stops working. This apparently was the case for shrews in the wild; their little hearts arrested when noisy craft flew overhead.

He turns and glances towards the front door which he can see from the utility room. The doorbell goes again. Giles finds he's unable to get up; as if he has been cemented to the chair. He is certain he's making enough effort to get out of his seat, or at least his brain is telling him he is, but he doesn't move. His legs are like jelly and his head like it's doubled in size. He wonders whether he is about to faint. If he is about to pass out he wishes that it happens quickly as it was sure to be better than the anxiety which has consumed him. The doorbell goes again, this time twice. Giles takes a deep breath and rises from the chair. He stands for a few seconds, ensuring that he can feel his legs then he starts to walk towards the front door. He gets to the door and is about to look through the door viewer but for some reason decides not to and boldly opens the door.

Stood in front of him is his mum who passed away to cancer over twenty years ago. This is the final straw for Giles whose legs now buckle underneath him and just before he drops to the floor, his head appears to grow larger than humpty dumpty's, he hopes as he uncontrollably drops to the floor in slow motion, that he doesn't shatter to pieces too like humpty dumpty and that is his final thought and any other conscious sense he has before the lights go out.

10

Giles wakes up with Scott over him. He realises that he's on his sofa at home. He steadily recollects what happened and calls out.

'Mum.'

'Here, drink this.' Scott offers Giles a drink of water.

'I saw my mum.' Giles pushes the glass of water away.

'I thought your mum died?' Scott ponders.

Giles now stops to think. He doesn't say another word. He realises that he may be sectioned if he carried on down the route he was going.

'Your mum died, right? Did you see your mum in a dream?'

'Yes...yes I must have.' Giles now takes the water and takes a sip.

'Are you okay? Found you on your doorstep with the door wide open. You must have had a seizure.' Scott touches Giles' forehead with the back of his hand.

'A little groggy but fine, thanks. How long have I been out for?'

'Well...from the time I found you, say about 30 minutes.'

Giles recalls what he saw. His mum was standing on his porch and she was smiling. She was looking alive as day. He could even smell her. She often smelt of figgy coconut, a fragrance Giles later found out was called Diptyque Philosykos. His mum had discovered the fragrance when holidaying in Rome and she had never stopped wearing it. Getting a whiff of this smell gave him a bittersweet memory of her. Smelling this whilst seeing his mum on the doorstep was too much for his brain to handle and he must have passed out. But did he really see her? Was it all in his mind? Giles did not know but he wanted it to be true. He wanted to believe he had seen her and why the hell not. It was his life and if he wanted to be seeing things then so be it. He just needed to be careful not to share it with anyone for fear of being locked away.

Giles pushes himself up from the sofa and sits in the corner and watches Scott. Then he remembers the CCTV footage.

'There is something I have to show you, just to make sure I'm not losing my mind.' Giles decides to take a chance.

'Okay, but you're sure you don't need some medical attention first.'

'No, honestly I'm fine.' Giles stands up determined not to sway.

'You remember when I asked over the phone if you remember seeing the person standing at my front door when we got back from lunch a few days back.'

'Thought you were kidding about that, yes I did see a young chap; I was just pulling your leg.'

'Yes...I know that.' Giles thinks about Paula and wonders whether to show Giles that footage and indeed find the footage of Habib too which he was sure was also an apparition of some sort. He was fairly certain of this now as that would explain his router playing up. It lost connectivity when Paula and Habib were present but not with Bright.

'Well, there was a reason I was asking you about that. There was a reason I was asking if you had seen the young man at my doorstep.'

'What do you mean?'

'There's no other way to explain this than just show you the CCTV footage.'

'Okayyyyyyy.' Scott checks Giles forehead again with the palm of his hand.

Giles gets up and goes to the utility room, Scott follows; a sense of caution in each step.

Giles switches the TV monitor on and turns on the computer. He clicks on the required icons and waits a few seconds and presses play.

'Watch this.' Giles says, looking at Scott.

Scott stares at the small TV monitor. He continues to watch and a silence exists that would render a whisper deafening.

Eventually Giles can be seen opening the door and talking as if to himself.

Scott inspects the screen and Giles.

'Is this you trying to get me back for pulling a prank on you about not seeing the young chap at your door?'

'No it's not; look at the date on the screen this was before me meeting the young chap at the front door.'

Giles can be seen opening the door wider and then closing the door. No doubt he was acting as if someone was present at the door. But there was no one.

'Okay, obviously you're pulling some kind of prank on me, cause there's no one there and you're just acting as if there is.

A good prank; I give you that; would have been better saved for Halloween but nonetheless a good prank.'

Giles realises Scott would not be convinced and if he carried on with this it would only potentially get worse for him. Straightjacket worse.

'Yeah, you're right, just playing with you.' Giles fakes a laugh.

'Are you sure you're alright and don't need someone to check you?'

'Yes, yes honestly, I'm fine. Would you like something to drink?'

'Cup of tea please.'

'Coming right up.' Giles comments uncharacteristically, again trying to eliminate the last few minutes in the utility room.

Giles struts out of the utility room with a repressed urgency.

Scott glances at the CCTV footage for another few seconds before turning around to follow Giles.

'Are you going to turn this off?' Scott holds on to the door to the utility room.

'Yes, I will later.' Giles picks up the kettle and fills it up. He places it in the electric portal and switches it on. He's trying desperately not to think about the recent events. He saw his mum and he saw someone at the door that wasn't physically there and the one solace he thought he had of Scott witnessing something strange on the CCTV footage had flunked, so he was pretty much on his own with the whole thing.

Scott picks up a pillow from the settee, hits it couple of times with the palm of his hand, places it on the back rest and sits down.

'So Giles, when are you going to get yourself a fella?'

Giles is thrown by this question, more so because Scott is a straight man. Nonetheless, this was perfect distraction and he was going to go along with it.

'Well, if there was a shop where I could go get one at a reasonable price, I wouldn't hesitate.'

Both men laugh out loud.

'Seriously though, you're at settlement age aren't you? Or is it different for gay men?'

'Why do people say a thing like this, like getting a partner is completely in your control?'

'Isn't it? You're a good looking sensitive man; you could have anyone if you wanted?'

'Oh, C'mon now...Anyone? I'm a middle aged gay man; most gay men my age are looking for someone younger, at least the better looking ones anyway. So that kinda narrows it down. Also people my age are becoming stuck in their ways and become less tolerant of breaking their habits of comfort.'

'True, perhaps, but it breaks even surely, most middle aged men will also know what they want, are more experienced in more ways than one.' Scott gives Giles a cheeky look which makes Giles blush.

'I would like to imagine that they are able to sieve out the fakes more easily and cherish integrity and honesty more in someone over physical beauty.' Scott adds.

'I wish that was true, men aren't like women. You will find a lot of hot women with older fat men but this trend is not quite so in the gay world. Men are more reliant on sexual aesthetics unfortunately, you better be hot when middle aged if not you don't get a look in. Men will automatically seek younger every time, pure genetic wiring. Fortunately, a lot of younger guys are now into older men, so all hope is not lost.'

'So you are looking for a younger guy?' Scott questions with the same cheeky grin.

'I didn't say that but yes I am, obviously someone that looks after themselves physically and mentally, so if the same age and is good looking then fine. But men my age tend to look a lot older, not to mention pessimistic, bitter and grumpy.'

'The ones you see on the dating apps anyway.' Scott says.

'Well it's mostly how people meet these days, way too much choice though and that's partly the problem. People always thinking they can do better, no patience, reduced tolerance. I find most dating apps soul destroying. I mean it's that bad that new words exist for people who waste your time like "ghosting" and "submarining."'

'What's that?'

'Ghosting describes someone who disappears after weeks or even months of chatting and texting and who so far as you're concerned you've developed an honest rapport with. A date is made to meet up and the person withdraws, goes cold and stops texting and calling. You never hear from them again.'

'Wow...and Submarines?'

'Sometimes the ghosts get back in touch, only to leave you hanging again when another time comes to meet. I mean I've done it myself, I don't go to the extreme of arranging a date and then disappearing, but sometimes after a few weeks of chatting you might realise that this person is not the one or someone else takes your fancy that's more promising.'

'Perhaps there is too much choice?' Scott proposes.

'That's definitely a factor, but more so it's the space that the apps can conjure up for you, the constant messing about and rejections almost become the norm and unless you're completely devoid of emotion and feelings then it is damn hard.'

'Sounds terrible.'

'It is.' Giles agrees and starts laughing. He often laughed at himself when he was playing into victim mode as it was so inauthentic to who he really was.

'It's not all bad; I've met some pretty amazing friends from these apps. I guess the trick is never to take the apps too seriously, it's a game and that's it. It's trying to attain the balance with attachment and detachment, whilst not getting disheartened, so as not to foil your chances of a decent meet.'

'The gay world sounds pretty tricky.'

'Yup.' Giles tries not to let himself become depressed by this sad fact.

'I'm sure it will happen when the time is right, right?'

'Yes, for now I try to enjoy my life and keep focused on writing and my friends – I have a lot to be grateful for, you included.'

There are a few moments of silence as both men take in the present.

'You know, since being single I realise this is exactly where I'm supposed to be. Learning to be at ease with myself when I'm alone has been a great learning. Ignoring the temptation of going on Grindr is the biggest challenge and I'm chuffed to bits I've not succumbed for over three years now.'

'Grindr is the gay dating app right?'

'Yea that's right, often soul destroying and packed full of ever increasing sexual deviants. People go to these apps for instant gratification with sex but it's the biggest illusion because you are never satisfied and it's a short term fix. The app is full of specious characters looking to use sex to bolster their waning spirits. Since meditating, I'm increasingly aware of the sense of aloneness that sometimes overwhelms me and that's when I'm tempted to meet someone for sex – so as to feel some kind of connection but it's the wrong kind. After the orgasm you return back to being empty in a matter of minutes, maybe hours if you're lucky.'

'I'm sure that heterosexual people do have these same feelings of deep loneliness – I reckon it's the distractions of kids' that make it more bearable. People do have this urge to turn to any kind of escape mainly because to just be with self is just so damn uncomfortable. I certainly don't think you're the only one Giles.'

'I'm sure I'm not, I guess some people are more aware of these feelings than others. Some just choose not to give it any attention. Deep thinkers like me unfortunately operate typically from the mind and it can be extremely exhausting. Thank God for meditation, otherwise my head could quite easily explode like the man in the movie "Scanners."'

'Well I must tell you being in a relationship isn't all rosy, it can be pretty damn hard. I would enjoy your peaceful times whilst you can.'

'Ha, it's funny you say that - I've always wished for nothing else than peace, peace and contentment in my life. That's all I've ever wanted. And then I wonder why I'm alone.'

Both men laugh.

'Well you best do some meditation when I have gone then.' Scott peers at Giles with a tender friendly smile.

After a few paused moments, Scott proclaims. 'Well, got things I must attend to.' He gets up and gives Giles a hug and then strides towards the front door.

'Yea, sure.' Giles mutters with some sadness in his voice. He could have done with the company for a bit longer as he felt somewhat vulnerable and alone. All the talk about loneliness probably hadn't helped. But he had decided since taking on meditation to be present to each moment, especially the uncomfortable ones and so he was going to do as Scott had advised and sit and meditate and be with his feelings, acknowledging his thoughts and continually coming back to his breath, sensations in his body, his weight on the chair, his heart beat which he could often feel throbbing in his chest. In time, calm always came, calm after the brainstorm, – it just needed a strong commitment to not run off with thoughts when they came but remain grounded in the now. Whilst it was a not-doing thing it was still a conscious decision to remain in the space and be okay with it.

'Thanks so much Scott.' Giles acknowledges, holding the front door.

'You're welcome buddy – I wasn't going to leave you on the porch for blackbirds to peck at was I?' He says smiling and turns around and swaggers back to the door and gives Giles another hug. He comes out from the embrace after a few seconds.

'Look after yourself.' Scott advises and drifts out the door.

Giles cannot help but feel like what Scott said was final, like he wasn't going to be seeing him again. Why did he have this thought – He had no idea but he did feel like it was bye for good. After a few moments of contemplating he puts it down to the after effects of the possible seizure. He closes the door gently behind him and gasps when he thinks he notices the router flashing but it stops flashing almost immediately. He's not sure whether he saw an intermittent flash or not. He strolls to the kitchen to get a drink of water. Suddenly he was parched. He gulps down the water and goes to sit on the sofa and proceeds to meditate.

He sits down with his back straight against the back of the chair and takes in six deep breathes and exhales from all his being. Finally on the last out breathe he closes his eyes and visualises scanning his body from the top of his head to the end of his toes. After doing this for a minute or so he starts to feel the sensations in his body, sensing the weight of his buttocks on the chair and his back against the back of the chair. After another couple of minutes he starts to focus on his breathing, counting as he breathes from one to ten and then returning to one. His mind interrupts now and again with thoughts of his mum, of the stranger that was at the door, of the various people that had been to see him and of Scott's last words as he left earlier. All lovely thoughts to hold onto but Giles acknowledges each of the cerebral processes, is aware that he is not the thought and returns to focussing on his breathing.

He remains in this space for over twenty minutes and does not want to come out of the blissful trance he has put himself into. Then he suddenly opens his eyes, with a stark realisation. He rushes to his mobile phone and calls Scott on his mobile. He is answered by a voicemail. Giles leaves a somewhat garbled message asking Scott to please call him back as soon as he gets the message. He is now riddled with anxiety. The words Scott said to him left ringing in his ears, comments from all the guests that had visited him in the last few weeks all ringing in his ears. He calls Scott's mobile phone again and again is answered by the voicemail. He tries to think if he has Scott's landline somewhere and rushes upstairs to check drawers – He searches in his bedroom and the spare room and finally as he is about to give up the search. He has always hated looking for something. He finds an old diary where he had written the number almost nine years ago. He picks the book up swiftly and rushes down the stairs again to call Scott on his landline. This time at least his wife might answer.

He rings and waits, it rings and rings and rings and no one answers, eventually a voice mail message breaks the silence. Giles puts the phone down in frustration. He picks up his mobile phone and checks to see if he's missed any calls or text messages from Scott but nothing. Giles' anxiety goes up a notch. He picks up his landline and calls Scott's residence again deciding that if there is no answer he was going to walk to his address. He was not going to be able to relax with the impending dread that was consuming him at the moment. What was going on through his head seemed absolutely ridiculous but he was not sure anything else made sense. Getting Scott on the phone would alleviate his fears and ethereal dread.

'Hello.' A female voice answers the phone.

'Hi, hello Giles here, can I speak to Scott please?'

'Oh, I'm afraid not, Scott went to an entrepreneur conference last night. It's Maggie here his wife, I have the call redirected to my mobile as I'm at work, can I help at all.'

Giles is lost for words; he does not know what to tell her.

'Hi Maggie, how are things?' He decides to speak as casually as possible. His heart is racing.

'Yea not bad thanks.'

'When did you last speak to Scott?'

'Well funnily enough he was supposed to call me last night when he got to the place his conference is at, of which the name now escapes me. But he hasn't, but then Scott can be a scatty brain sometimes so...'

Again Giles is dumbfounded; he struggles to get his brain to work.

'Is everything okay?' Maggie checks with concern in her voice.

'Yes, yes everything is fine; I just need to get hold of Scott. I have tried him on his mobile and he's not answering.'

'Probably because he's in the conference, he won't be able to use his phone whilst at the meeting.'

'Of course...Did he go by car?' Giles tries desperately to pretend that he hadn't seen Scott just an hour ago. How could he tell his wife that he was at his home, when she thinks he's attending a conference?

'Yes he drove up, it's over a four hour journey which is why I wasn't so fussed that he hadn't called me last night. He must have been zonked.'

'Yes, yes.' Giles is befuddled and tries to calm his racing heart.

'Are you sure you're alright?' Maggie quizzes again with concern in her voice.

'Yes, sorry, yes I am, please let me know the moment you hear from Scott, I'd appreciate that very much.'

'Okay I will do. In fact I will call him now; you've kinda got me worried.'

Giles comes off the phone and does not know quite what to do with himself. He can't stop the thought racing through his mind. He tries to still his mind using his meditation practise but in this instance is unable to. He peers over at the side table that is besides his sofa and spots a book he did not see before. He can't remember who gave him the book. Was it one of his visitors? On the front cover of the book are the words. "You need do nothing but connect with others and yourself."

Strange title for a book he thinks but is mainly blown away by the poignancy of the words.

In a flash he remembers the name that Flora gives him at the event that Scott organised.

'Mr Conway.'

Why didn't he note that name – it had to be Tyler Conway, the name that Habib had warned him about. He had to get in touch with Flora immediately. Habib had asked him to act swiftly. He should have asked Flora to confirm the first name, why had he been so distracted by Flora. Every moment that passed increased his assuredness that the unpleasant man at the evening event was Tyler Conway. He grabs his phone and starts to search in Google for therapists under the name of Flora. He sieves to the back of his mind the joke about 'the rapist.' In no time he finds the name of a counselling and therapy service with Flora as a leading Psychotherapist. He instantly dials the number and waits whilst listening to his beating heart.

Now, not only was he to deal with his impending dread over the fate of Scott but he was also worried for Flora. He wasn't sure which to deal with first and decides to deal with both situations simultaneously.

'Hello?' Flora answered the phone.

'Hi, hi...Flora?'

'Yes this is Flora.'

'Oh, thank god.' Giles exhales air that he had forgotten to.

'Who's this?'

'Oh...Sorry its Giles, met you earlier this evening at Scott's event.'

'Oh, hi Giles – it's weird that you call because there was an incident at Mrs Conway's residence. You know the man I was talking to...'

'Yea I know, what happened?' Giles braces himself, his heart beating even faster.

'Well, I was concerned about his wife after his behaviour at Scott's event and so I decided to call their home. After a long while his wife did answer the phone to my relief, but she was distressed. She said that he had been round and was ranting and raving about teaching Scott a lesson for kicking him out of his party. He said he knew exactly where to find him and left the house in a rage.'

'Did he say where he was going to meet Scott?'

'Unfortunately not.'

'Okay Flora, please call the police straight away– I think something awful may have happened to Scott. Tell the police his full name is Scott Pritchard and that he could be in a lot of danger. Ask the police to please go to his address which is 65 Claydon Street.' Giles does not need confirmation from Flora about the name Tyler Conrad. He is a hundred percent convinced.

'Oh my god, why? What do you think has happened?'

'Haven't got time to explain Flora, please call the police immediately I'm going to the address now.' Giles hangs up the phone and knows in his heart that Scott is more than likely dead which is why he saw him. He now knows for sure that all the people that have been visiting apart from the little old lady and maybe Bright have been ghosts. Seeing his mum was not some dream, he had genuinely seen her too. That in itself is confirmation. He knows it's absurd but nonetheless is certain that is what has been happening. One of them had warned him about Tyler Conrad and he had been slow to act and now something awful could have happened to Scott. He wasn't sure how he was going to live with himself. He grabs his keys and rushes out the door. He runs to Scott's address, hoping that Flora hadn't delayed with calling the police because he was frightened for his life too.

Giles runs down the street, his heart racing almost in synchrony to his racing feet. He reaches the address and witnesses a flickering light from the window. Momentarily, he believes the house has been set on fire. Scott has set the whole house in flames; perfect way to get rid of someone perhaps. He then realises that the shimmering orangey light is coming from a lit candle by the window. Giles reaches the porch and notices the door is ajar. His heart takes a double flipping beat as if to counterbalance the fact that it had been beating ever so fast, a combination of him running and the adrenaline flowing through his system.

'Hello. Scott!'

Giles calls out whilst pushing the door fully open and he calls out again.

'Scott, hello!'

Suddenly a thud and crash stops Giles in his tracks. A black cat dashes out of the kitchen meowing as it stealthily avoids obstacles whilst maintaining its speed. Giles had forgotten that Scott had a cat. He puts his hand to his heart wondering how many double flips his heart will be able to take before it completely packs in. He wonders whether to go back outside and wait for the police to arrive. This was not some book he was writing where his character would have to go into the house to create thrill and suspense; this was his life, which may turn out to be near ending if he did not rethink the heroics!

Giles turns around and strides back towards the front door which is still open. He wonders what scared the cat and if indeed it was something or if the cat freaked out about him being in the house. Cats do weird shit. As he reaches the front door he spots the cat sat on the wooden fence bordering the premise. The cat stares sternly at the house. Giles wonders why the cat is so spooked. It doesn't appear there is anyone in the house. He walks out and listens for any sirens and cannot hear anything. He decides to investigate around the perimeter of the house. Thick shrub borders the perimeter; they have been trimmed to be in alignment with the window sills. He peers through the windows as he strays around the house. The building is a similar layout to his so he knows which rooms to expect where. He does know that Scott had decided to use one of the downstairs small rooms as storage for all his electronic equipment; whereas he had turned his into a utility slash study.

So far no sign of anyone, he would have expected Scott's wife to be back home too. She was a school teacher and had an uncanny way with kids as she was able to effortlessly engage with them and always knew when a child was telling lies to the extent they didn't bother trying. The kids respected her implicitly because she was always her word and put boundaries in place which made the kids feel safe. Giles never could understand why some parents couldn't fathom this basic parenting skill.

He continues walking around the house and notices something in the corner of his eye, a movement which he couldn't quite make out. He thinks maybe it's the cat and looks back at the fence where the cat had perched staring at the house and it was still there, albeit less alert. Giles looks back at the window to a little room which Scott also used for storage and focuses his eyes to see if he could make sense of the movement he had seen. He pushes through the shrub bordering the wall to get a better look and suddenly stops in his tracks. He feels his head swell and his legs feel like marshmallows in a powered microwave. He stands still and for a few moments his brain does not function, his neurons seize to fire.

Lying on the floor struggling was Scott, he was tied up. His ankles are tied together and his hands tied behind his back. He was struggling to get loose. He looks up at Giles with intense fear in his eyes and he starts to nod his head furiously whilst still staring at his hopeful saviour. Giles' heart slowly starts to feed some blood back to his legs allowing room for his brain to function, he then sees in the other corner of his eye another figure standing and pouring something out of a jerry can. He doesn't take long to figure out what was going on. He is about to tap on the window but then decides against it. Tyler had not realised he was there and he was going to take advantage of this. He carefully disentangles himself from the shrub and makes his way back to the front door.

Giles reaches the front door with caution; he wonders why he cannot hear any sirens yet and wonders if sirens were just for the movies. If the police were attending a crime scene for real would there be sirens? Would they want to alert the criminals they were on their way? As he was pondering, partly for distraction as his adrenaline was drowning his system, he hears the sirens and they sound close. Perhaps they did not have to put them on all the way and then switched them on as they got closer to the scene? Again he wondered and then thought how silly that he didn't actually know. He reaches for the door and pushes it wider open and out of nowhere takes a deep breath and bellows.

'The police are on their way, so I'd scamper if I was you!!' Giles shouts hoping the intruder will go out the back door instead of confronting him at the front. He hears a shuffle and something hitting the floor hard but not breaking and then the sound of the back door open and slam hard.

'Scott!' Giles shouts walking swiftly to the room where he saw him tied up. For a split second, he thinks what if the back door slamming shut was a trick to get him to come into the house. He stops in his tracks in the hallway and listens intently. He hears the sirens which are getting even closer, definitely coming to this address. He starts to walk again but this time paces himself, the sound of the sirens was not quite enough to give him the courage to move as swiftly as he was initially doing. He continues to listen intently for any sound, consciously filtering out the sound of the sirens.

'Scott.' He calls out again, this time a lot more restrained. His heart is racing and he envisions Scott on the floor with his throat slit. He shakes his head frantically trying to get the image out of his head. 'Scott.' He calls again as he reaches the doorway to the room.

As he approaches the open door and looks into the room he sees instantly Scott is curled up on the floor in foetal position. He is facing away from him and looks still. Giles thinks the worse and walks over to him, heart beating a lot faster and just as he is about to allow the image of Scott lying on the floor with a slit throat cross over his cerebrum again. Scott moves and muffles something. He had been gagged, probably when Giles had opened the front door and called out his name. He turns Scott around, it's obvious he had been crying and he pulls the dirty rag from his mouth and starts to untie the ropes that were cutting into his wrists and ankles. There is a big wound on the side of his head. Giles figures he must have been knocked out cold. There is a strong aroma of petrol and Scott appears to be drenched in it including the dirty rag that he had pulled from his mouth.

'Don't worry Scott, the police are here.' Giles says whilst yanking at the rope on his ankles.

'I came to you; I came to you in a dream.' These are the only words that Scott could muster. He says it whilst drying his eyes.

'Hun!'

It's the voice of Scott's wife at the front door.

11

Sticky humidity fills the atmosphere, the type of atmosphere that keeps you up at night. The type of climate that may get bachelors out of their beds so as to find some solace, some release from the horniness exacerbated by hot humid weather. Several men drive up and down a well known street for picking up prostitutes. The street lights emit an orange hue over the main road, in a way exacerbating the already warmed up environment. Sound of hard core music emerges from a club nearby which is set in the basement of one of the buildings. The bass of the music rattles and echoes off all conductive surfaces.

Several women all scantily dressed hurdle up in a street corner chatting loudly. On another corner, is a lady also scantily dressed stood on her own. She is texting and appears stressed. She glimpses around occasionally as if expecting someone and after a few minutes she finishes her text and presses send. She puts the phone in her handbag and adjusts her burgundy skirt and takes another look around. The ladies in the group look in her direction and all mutter to themselves and start laughing loudly. The lady with the burgundy skirt takes in a deep breath and slowly turns her back to the group. She examines the street and admires the way the orange light from the street lamps appears to shimmer down; polarised light filtering through smoke and fog. She adjusts her skirt again and forces a smile as a dark blue BMW quietly pulls up next to her. She peers at the car which has tinted windows and she smiles some more whilst waiting for the window to be wound down. The side window goes down and a man with a bushy moustache leans out and asks how much.

'Depends what you want.' The woman resists the urge to adjust her skirt again.

The man looks her up and down and then turns around to look at the group of women who are now hurriedly walking to designated spots in the street, some cursing at having missed an opportunity. The man peeks at the woman that has been singled out.

'I'd like a slow blow job, depending how good you are will determine whether I fuck you or not. Money is not an issue.' The man adjusts his groin.

Suddenly another car pulls up and the other women are alarmed and start to run. It takes a while for the lady in the burgundy skirt to realise it's the police. The BMW skids off leaving a trail of exhaust smoke which envelopes the woman he was about to pick up. She waves her hands through the smoke which may have concealed her from the police if she hadn't panicked. She starts to run and scampers into the main street, looking back as she does so. The police car still cruises, but in her direction. The woman continues to run, grateful that she hadn't decided to wear the high heeled shoes she normally wears on a Tuesday night. The last couple of months when customers were scarce the other women had always taken delight in telling her 'See you next Tuesday.'; then laughing hysterically like a pack of deranged hyenas. She had known what they meant and always ignored them. She had thought that whilst she may well be a lady of the night there was no need to be so uncouth. She would never use the "C" word and especially thought it was crass for women to say it when it was a derogatory term for the most sensitive part of their anatomy.

Her phone starts to ring and she starts to rummage in her handbag whilst still running down the street. She is unaware that she has now ventured into the road from the pavement. She looks up and is temporarily blinded by glaring illumination from headlights moments before she is hit by a car and flung threw the air with great velocity, smashing into a clothes shop window and splayed into a hurdle of scantily dressed mannequins, broken glass all around her.

She stays still unable to feel any part of her body; she is unaware of the increasing pool of blood she is lying in. Instead she is fixated on a small piece of glass that is lodged in her hand. She also faintly discerns the scattered mannequins around her and she can almost hear them laughing at her hysterically. She is terribly thirsty and has never experienced thirst like it. She didn't think the body was efficient at telling you when it needed water anyway, very often going by the colour of your pee to signal to you that you needed to be hydrated. This time however, her body was telling her loud and clear that it needed water. To say she was parched was an understatement. Nonetheless, she remained still and could not remember any time where she had felt so much peace. Her often busy mind seemed to have slowed right down, so much so she was only aware of where she was and at one with her thirst. An all encompassing peace seemed to swallow her up and she thought of brief moments in her life where she had fleeting seconds of immense peace and contentment, very brief indeed.

In those moments she had somehow detached from her mind but of course as soon as she realised her space, the mind was activated again and the moment of tranquillity was gone. This time however as she lay on the tarmac floor in a pool of blood that camouflaged her skirt, she realises that the moment of peace was maintained. Her mind had ceased to intellectualise, there was nothing to compartmentalise. She lay there and was comfortable in the nothingness and had faith in whatever outcome she was to face. She was probably going to die, as it could not be a good sign that she could not feel any part of her body and the fact that she was so terribly thirsty could only mean one thing. She was losing a lot of blood. She allowed herself to be wrapped up in the warm light that she now envisioned. She smiled at the realisation of the mind, the paradox of it all. She had often resisted and beaten herself up over how much her mind tormented her. But now she realised that the mind had to be the way it was. Chaos had to exist for there to be peace. It was just the way it was. The resolve was being with the chaos of the mind, embracing it, noticing it without judgement, whilst observing how you feel, all the body sensations, acknowledging your surroundings and of course your breathing. Here she was doing it effortlessly; it had taken for her to crash into a shop window at 30 miles an hour for her to finally get it, but she was relieved for this enlightenment, even though her life was ending.

She was content as she lay on the floor flooded by headlights possibly from the car that had hit her. It's all she had ever wanted to feel, an all encompassing peace and to not be driven by anxiety and over thinking. She smiles and allows the warm light to engulf her but not before knowing she had to pay a visit to a guy called Giles.

12

Giles sits in his favourite armchair underneath the skylight – it's been months since he last saw Scott. The experience Scott had gone through had changed him considerably, as facing death often did to people. Scott was convinced that he had died and had visited Giles at the house. Giles had chosen not to confirm to him that this was true, he decided to tell him another time, mainly because he had continued to see his mum and he wasn't sure he wanted to share that and the fact he had seen others who had visited him at the house. He was quite certain that Scott would be fine with the news, especially since he believed wholeheartedly that he had died and visited Giles at home. But for some reason he decided not to tell him yet, as he would have to tell him everything.

Scott had become very spiritual, embarking on voluntary work where he was helping people that had been through traumatic episodes in their life. This took up most of his time and so there was hardly any time for him to see friends although when he did meet up with his mates he was the most present to their company he had ever been. Cherishing each and every moment like it was his last. Giles missed him but was happy for him at the same time. He was happy for him because he knew that having a purpose and immersing in it was the most content place to be.

Giles had a box of pictures and was rummaging through them, reminiscing in his high school days. A friend of his called Egbuke who he was very close to had unfortunately died from a rare cancer. He was only twenty when he passed away. His family had moved over to Nigeria from USA. He and Egbuke were inseparable; he was the first guy he kissed, he was the one person that gave him some sense of normality whilst dealing with his father's violent and promiscuous behaviour.

Egbuke had often given him some wise words that had always comforted him. It was as if a divine force was using his body to produce consoling words.

Once when he father was being violent and had decided to pile up both he and his sisters clothes, setting them alight in a rage over the kitchen been left dirty. Egbuke came to the locked gate and took hold of Giles hands and looked him in the eye and asked why. Giles never understood why he asked him that, it wasn't as if he had any control over his dad's behaviour, what could he do? Egbuke looked him in the eye and asked why he let this carry on and Giles never got it until a lot later on in his life when he read the book called 'The Secret.' As he was remembering this he recalls the intensity of his eyes and remembered those of Bright, the teenager that had visited him. Then he recalls something else – the name 'Egbuke' meant 'Bright' in the Igbo language where Egbuke originated from. It was highly likely that Bright was born right about the time that Egbuke passed away. A kind of excitement never before experienced rushes all over Giles. He grabs his phone with haste and Googles the word reincarnation.

13

Giles sits in a Waterstones bookshop signing a new book he had written entitled "Eliminating segregation in society." He was proud of this book as it was borne from the most research he had ever done and enjoyed it thoroughly. He had promised Habib that he would write something to help people understand terrorism from both sides and that had required a lot of research into the human condition, integrity and in a sense, societal blindness to other realities. He had spent three years working on the book and it had resulted in a few sleepless nights because some of the material was controversial and it was going to cause some people to be outraged but he was going to find every way to publish it if his life depended on it, because he had promised Habib.

Three years ago he had been in the library and spotted a short story by Joseph Jaworski which read like this:

"Tell me the weight of a snowflake?" A coal mouse asked a wild dove.

"Nothing more than nothing." Was the answer.

"In that case, I must tell you a marvellous story," the coal mouse said.

"I sat on the branch of a fir, close to its trunk, when it began to snow – not heavily, not in a raging blizzard – no just like in a dream, without a wound and without any violence. Since I

did not have anything better to do, I counted the snowflakes settling on the twigs and needles of my branch. Their number was exactly 3,741,952. When the 3,741,953rd dropped onto the branch, nothing more than nothing as you say – the branch broke off."

Having said that, the coal mouse scurried away.

The dove, since Noah's time an authority on the matter, thought about the story for a while and finally said to herself, "Perhaps there is only one person's voice lacking for peace to come to the world."

Not only was this story comforting in the knowledge that no positive action by a human being was ever wasted but hidden was the profound hint at the beauty of paying attention to the present. If the coal mouse hadn't decided to count the snowflakes, a task most people would have dreaded for the sheer tediousness of it, the little creature would never have picked up the wisdom nature was giving it.

The story makes him remember what Habib had told him when he came to visit and he decides to look up terrorism in Syria. He unveils a small article printed over nine years ago about a little girl who had been killed in a school following an explosion. In a picture he later finds in the archives, he observes a man holding a bloodied young girl in his arms and crying. Giles knew straight away this man was Habib, the man who had come to see him in the early hours of the morning and enlightened him on a taboo subject, the man who had somehow instilled in him a fearlessness to approach life more powerfully than he had ever imagined. He later discovered when reading the article further that Habib had committed suicide soon after finding his little sister dead after a stray bomb hit a school in the middle of nowhere.

THE END

Printed in Great Britain
by Amazon